HOLIDAYS

HOLIDAYS

Short Stories by Lisa Ruffolo

with artworks by Kathryn Wright

Minnesota Voices Project Number 29

NEW RIVERS PRESS 1987

Copyright © 1987 by Lisa Ruffolo
Library of Congress Catalog Card Number: 86-63557
ISBN: 0-89823-086-1
All rights reserved
Design and Typesetting: Peregrine Publications, St. Paul
Backcover photo: Allan Grossman

Grateful acknowledgment is made to the editors of the following publications for the permission to reprint some of the stories in this collection (sometimes under different titles and in somewhat different form): *Northern New England Review, Real Fiction, South of the North Woods, The Beloit Fiction Journal, Montana Review, New Oregon Review,* and *Mississippi Mud.*

Holidays has been published with the aid of grants from the Jerome Foundation, the Dayton Hudson Foundation, the First Bank System Foundation, and the National Endowment for the Arts (with funds appropriated by the Congress of the United States).

New Rivers Press books are distributed by:

The Talman Company   and   Bookslinger
150-5th Avenue   213 E. 4th St.
New York, NY 10011   St. Paul, MN 55101

Holidays has been manufactured in the United States of America for New Rivers Press, Inc. (C. W. Truesdale, editor/publisher), 1602 Selby Ave., St. Paul, MN 55104 in a first edition of 1,200 copies.

CONTENTS

To My Family

HALLOWEEN

I WORK AS THE ENGLISH TEACHING INTERN at a private day school in New England. It is the first week of classes, and the low late-summer sun masks the inevitable chill of fall. The social studies intern, Roland Tartan, told me he isn't sure he wants to be a social studies teacher. Roland is unfortunately pear-shaped and pompous, and the skin between his upper lip and nose always seems to be sweating. The students have already invented derogatory nicknames for him — Mr. Two Ton, Mr. Rotund, and, of course, Plaid. Roland stopped me today between classes. He explained he was having a bad day. "Francie, I never should have dropped my Journalism major," he said, opening his small hands. "These kids don't even read the newspapers. I wanted to be a columnist, you know." I smiled — Roland had concealed desires! I said I was sure that some columnists secretly wanted to teach high school social studies.

I haven't yet made a firm decision to be an English teacher. I heard about this program from a friend who enthusiastically applied for an internship and didn't receive one. She made teaching sound fulfilling and important. You get to stand in front of interested students and talk about books, she said. What could be better? During orientation, the head of the English department told me that if I thought of myself as a veteran teacher, the students would perceive me as one. He was filling in a seating chart with his neat handwriting. Perhaps you'd like to sit in on some of my classes this week, he said. He printed INTERN in an extra square on his seating chart.

Here is some of the advice the old pros in the English department have given me: If you think the students are not keeping up with the readings, assign an in-class essay for the next day. Don't forget about spelling and vocabulary quizzes — the parents like them. Be sure to write on the board and ask students to read aloud. These are some of the hallmarks of a good teacher.

I think I am personable, but not very social. I occasionally squander part of my meager intern salary on a bottle of good white Bordeaux, then settle in on a Saturday night to correct eleventh grade papers. At home, I heat or chill plates even for crackers and cheese, snip articles from magazines and send them to my sisters, and turn on the single lamp in my bedroom to reread letters from old friends. I think of myself as a young World War II widow. There is even an ornate gas heater in my apartment.

I'm the kind of person others confide in. Jacquie Bloom, the Phys Ed intern, came to my classroom during a free period and closed the door. She asked me if I could be discreet, then told me that she was secretly involved with the trumpet-playing music intern. He thinks she looks like Brigitte Bardot. They started seeing one another after he showed up on the soccer field one afternoon and yelled, "Hey, Brigitte." Jacquie blew her whistle and tossed her long ponytail. After the students left, he followed her into the locker room to kiss her with his swollen lips. Jacquie looks flushed and lovely as she tells me this — having a secret life becomes her.

In class, Oswald Dow explains he couldn't finish his assignment because he'd been kicked out of study hall. Should I ask him to write an in-class essay? Give him a spelling or vocabulary quiz? Make him read aloud? What would a real teacher do, I wonder. I tell him to hand in the assignment — a paraphrase of a scene from *Macbeth* — the next day. I don't call on him at all during class.

At the beginning of October, we have an inservice on right brain-left brain theories in education. Two professors from Boston University make the presentation. They explain that by emphasizing certain activities, drawing for example, formerly weak students can be transformed into strong, confident ones. After the presentation, we all attend a party the head of the upper school traditionally hosts. Mature seniors are asked to hang coats and serve food. All of the veteran teachers drink Scotch and soda. This is the second big party of the year. At the first party in September, a middle school teacher mistook me for a senior, and asked me to bring her clean silverware. This time, one of the Boston University professors joins me on a couch and asks me what I teach. He *assumes* I'm not a student. I tell him I would like copies of his right brain-left brain articles.

I'm not getting much sleep this year. All of my old friends from home call me after eleven, when they can afford the rates. They are making their way through graduate school, or finishing incompletes from last semester. They tell me they are studying and drinking Beck's beer at the Ace Club or the Pulse. I cannot remember the faces of the classmates they gossip about. I tell them I think teaching is important. It can change lives.

It is Parents Night. We meet the parents of our students in our classrooms; they sit in their son's or daughter's desk, wear name tags, and cluck over the compositions I've posted on the bulletin board. More than one parent confesses he or she was an English teacher before marrying. The mother of one of my best students is a single parent. She stays after the other parents leave and leans against the blackboard. "Have you been to Northampton," she asks me. "You'd like its progressive atmosphere." Then she explains that some of the other teachers disapprove of Northampton, all those alternative after-hours places.

The Spanish teacher used to be a nun. Now she raises two rambunctious young boys with her husband, an automobile dealer. She met him in Costa Rica, then left the convent, and decided to be a teacher in America. Now she is one of the most popular teachers in the school. She wears red shoes and carries a briefcase. She smokes small cigars at the faculty parties. What happened? Did she walk out of the convent and into a Costa Rican tobacco shop? Or did the changes metamorphosize when she moved to America? Did she, for example, wear red shoes with conservative black skirts, or smoke cigars and go to Mass every morning — part dull caterpillar, part gaudy butterfly?

I think I am making progress with my classes. After I assigned *Catcher in the Rye*, Frank Barlow, one of my most incorrigible students, came to class early. "This is the best thing I have ever read," he declared. His sidekick, Jimmy Derns, slouched to his desk and said, "My mother can't stand it. I'm becoming Holden Caulfield."

As a child, I wanted to be a close friend of one of the Beatles. Then, when Linda Eastman met Paul McCartney, I wanted to be a photographer. As recently as last summer I thought about applying for law school.

It is almost Halloween. The students are changing before my eyes. The seniors especially seem more purposeful and serious. Some of the boys are growing beards, and look genuinely handsome. The other day, a senior who had been aloof and troublesome for weeks met with me to discuss her college essay. She was applying to the same college from which I graduated. I told her about life in the dorms, registration, professors. She blinked and said I seemed like a different person to her now. It hadn't occurred to her that I had just left the world she was about to enter. Then she told me she wanted to be a teacher, maybe of French, or English, or both.

I am sprucing up my classroom with potted geraniums, colorful postcards, and maps. Some of the teachers have been here for fifteen, twenty years. They are still amazed that students prefer sitting out on the front lawn to watching their chemistry demonstrations. I wonder if I could teach that long — remember all those names of older brothers and sisters, come up with fresh paper topics after teaching *Ethan Frome* every winter for ten years. Would I be cynical and stultified, or wise and experienced?

Soon I'll be assigning my eleventh graders one of my favorite books — *The Adventures of Huckleberry Finn*. My favorite scene is when, during a thick fog, Huck falls off the raft and into the Mississippi. He sneaks back onto the raft, and lets Jim think he is lost on the river. Jim is frantic without him, and the next morning Huck impishly tells Jim that he must have dreamed the fog. Jim realizes Huck is enjoying a joke at his expense, and retreats with his dignity until Huck humbles himself. The best thing about this chapter is that you can see Huck changing from a kid on the run to Jim's friend. You can't underline the words that tell you this, but Huck is a different person after this episode.

As an intern/teacher, I am really once removed from being a student, and once removed from being a teacher. I see students awkwardly push packs of cigarettes into their lockers, and hear teachers in the Faculty Lounge complain about a student's attitude. I can, on any given weekend, be invited to a party at a student's house where the parents are out of town, or be asked to chaperone the Freshman dance.

Teaching interns, like full-fledged teachers, are necessarily frugal. I feel even more like a World War II widow when I run a pair of stockings and know I can't afford another pair until the end of the month. At the beginning of the year, I wore my old college clothes: denim skirts and crew-neck sweaters. Now I am ready to buy something more professional: blazers and blouses.

Yesterday a group of popular girls joined me for lunch. They identified teachers who had once been interns — Mr. Taylor and Ms. Schrank — and complained that Mr. Tartan graded unfairly. Then one told me she liked my class. It seemed I was in a fog at first, she confessed. They were going to give me a trucker's hat printed with the words "Space Cadet." But now I seem to know what's going on. They'd have to give me a different hat, perhaps one with "William Shakespeare" or "Mark Twain" printed on it.

On Halloween night, all of the interns decide to have a costume party, a Sublimated Desires party. Jacquie wears petticoats and a hooped skirt — I guess she secretly wants to be a southern belle. I whisk about in something I found at a secondhand shop — a Miss Jean Brodie kind of cape. The music intern calls Jacquie Scarlet, and follows her from the kitchen to the dining room to the living room.

I sip my Scotch and soda and remember an incident from the night before. Jacquie and I stopped at a bar in Amherst and ordered tacos and beer. The pot-bellied bartender asked to see my driver's license. Look, I said, that's not necessary. I'm a teacher at the school up the road. I stared at him as severely as I've stared at Oswald Dow, and he popped open two bottles of beer. They were cold and delicious.

I am impressed with the costumes the other interns have devised for the Halloween party. Someone is wearing gold chains and a shirt open to the waist. He wants to be Bob Guccione. Roland Tartan wears black robes and a white collar. At first I think he wants to be a nun, like the Spanish teacher, until he tells me he has been accepted at the Boston University law school. Roland has grown a blond moustache, and looks surprisingly distinguished.

We are all changing after the fog. My students, for example, are becoming adults. The other day, one said she didn't care if this English class helped her get into college; she liked to learn! I wanted to stop class and parade her around the school. Instead, I looked over at my reflection in the window. A smiling woman in a blue blazer seemed to be floating among the November clouds. When I looked back at my students, I thought, I am a teacher.

YOU'LL LOSE THEM
BEFORE THANKSGIVING

I CAN'T DECIDE WHAT TO WEAR: my closet is filled with faded Indian-print wrap-around skirts, but no pumps or plaid dresses. I push a Talking Heads album onto the stereo, trot and twist around the apartment in only my bra and slip. When I flick my head and begin to sing, droplets from my wet hair spatter the furniture. "Great," Gretchen cries from her bedroom. She jumps out and twirls around me and the furniture in a bright gypsy skirt. We are going to be late for the all-faculty party.

"Panic," Gretchen said when I asked her why she took the job at Ford Country Day. "Post-collegiate panic." We both teach 10th and 11th grade English. It is our first week at Ford Country Day.

On the way to the party, I open the window of Gretchen's car and stick my head out the window, hoping my hair will dry in the damp autumn air.

Gretchen laughs. "Mastiff or rottweiler or spitz," she says.

"Huh?" I ask, drawing my head in the car.

"That's what you look like. One of those dogs."

"Oh, c'mon," I say. "I can't even spell those names. How could I be one?" I smooth down my hair and shake out my skirt. I have decided to wear a turquoise dirndl with bells in the hem and a gauzy white blouse. I will have to walk around the party slowly. That, or stay seated.

"Arf," Gretchen barks. "Arf, arf. That's what a rottweiler sounds like." Gretchen is from New England. Her family raised a lot of dogs.

At the party, only the art teacher will talk to Gretchen and me. Our department head nibbles cauliflower and cherry tomatoes, rolling them first in the cheese dip. Every time he selects a vegetable, the intricate star design formed by an outer ring of green peppers collapses. A history teacher and two other English teachers, all in earth-tone sport jackets, speak to our department head earnestly.

"I bet they think we're gay," I say to Gretchen. We have been inseparable since we met three weeks ago. A faculty wife arranged for us to be roommates. No one believes we hadn't met before. "Be true, be true, be true," she replies. We have been rereading *The Scarlet Letter.*

Bert, the art teacher, smiles and jingles my skirt. "Oh, no, my dear," he says, mimicking a fluty-voiced matron. "No, no, no, no, no." Bert, whose full name is Albert, wanted to be called Al last year. Coach Bucks explained this to me yesterday at lunch. "Al, Bert," Coach Bucks said, stabbing a piece of chicken cutlet. "He's a fruitcake no matter what you call him."

After my third glass of warm white wine, I get brave and approach the headmaster, Winston McAffey. He is an Episcopalian minister. The students who like him call him "The Rev." Those who don't call him "The Rave." This is the kind of detail students let slip to new teachers during the first week of class.

"Hey, Mare," the headmaster says. I don't like it when someone shortens my name. My name is Marie, which is short enough as it is.

"Say, Angie's the star of American Lit," I lie. Angie is the headmaster's daughter. He looks up hopefully and his wife appears at his elbow, pushing up the sleeves of her cardigan sweater. I immediately regret my drunken lie, but see something like sorrow on the headmaster's face, so I continue.

"She's very sensitive to character and quick to respond to others' opinions," I improvise.

The headmaster pauses and munches thoughtfully on a canape. "Glad to hear you say that. No one else has picked up on it. Her sensitivity. Perhaps American literature is the answer." He pauses. "Dear?" he asks his wife.

"Angie works hard," her mother reports.

Angie is mysteriously unpopular. She wears all the right clothes and plays all the right sports, but can't relax or smile. "Oh, forget it," she replied the first day, and crumbled the dittos on her desk. I had asked the students to name a book they loved.

"Fifteen years, Winston." Don Krepelich, the math teacher, is handing the headmaster a beer. "Don't you think it's time for a raise?" Don's giggle sounds unnatural coming from a big man with a dark beard.

I look down and see a run crawling up my pale blue stockings. "Let's split this pop stand," I say when I find Gretchen.

"Panic," she says again. "First week panic."

I assign the juniors Hawthorne's "Ethan Brand." "Before you read this," I say, "let's talk about sin." I hold a piece of chalk as I would hold a cigarette. "Think carefully before you answer my question. Okay. 'Ethan Brand' is a story about a man in search of the unpardonable sin. What do you think the unpardonable sin is?" I am certain this will generate a discussion to last for the rest of class. Twenty-five minutes remain.

Everyone stares at me. This is my quiet class. "Anybody," I say. "Jump right in." I listen anxiously, honestly curious.

Finally a tall boy twirling a cord of the venetian blinds says, "Your parents hiring some old maid to housesit while they go to Hiltonhead for the weekend." The class titters dutifully.

"Mmmm," I reply. "Sounds pretty pardonable. How 'bout some other ideas?"

"Raping a pregnant unwed mother," a pale girl declares.

"Abortion," a surly boy states.

"Lying."

"Not being nice to everyone whenever you can."

"Being stuck with your parents when you think you belong with someone else," Angie says.

A hard rain silvers the windows, and my students turn noisily to see the storm's first bright branch of lightning. "Okay," I say. "Hold it. Hold it right there. Read the story. Think about unpardonability. Page 126." Thunder booms. The bell will ring in eighteen minutes. "You can go now," I say with relief.

Later, in the teacher's lounge, my department head speaks to me about dismissing class early. "Start tough," he advises me and adjusts his glasses. "Otherwise you'll lose them by Thanksgiving."

Jeff calls me on the phone, long-distance. "The Frantic-Frenzy Room," he explains. Jeff is my boyfriend. He lives four hundred miles away. The Frantic-Frenzy Room is a reading room in the library where he studies psychology. I have been trying to reach Jeff for days. "One night I got home at three a.m. The other night I didn't get home at all. My stomach's pitted from the coffee."

"Crappo," I say. "Where's Sarah been these days?"

Last year, during troubled February, Jeff was late for a dinner date. I went over to his house, let myself in with the key, and fell asleep on his couch. He never showed up that night. I unplugged the water pump and pulled all the algae out of his tropical fish tank. Jeff loved those fish. Later, he explained it to me. "I was at my friend Sarah's house. It was convenient to stay there." Jeff saw a lot of Sarah that February, and I lost a lot of weight and sleep. Nearly every day I told him that what he was doing was wrong, unforgivably wrong.

"I can't talk to you when you're like this," Jeff says.

"Let's go for a ride," I say to Gretchen after I hang up. "Let's go see if this town has a ghetto." I grab my disk camera, squint at Gretchen in the view finder.

Gretchen and I drive away from the suburbs, and follow the streets until the asphalt crumbles.

I snap pictures of abandoned cars and railyards. "I should have been a photographer," I say.

"I should have been a truck driver," Gretchen says. "I love driving."

"Maybe I'll look Jenkins up when we get home." I had an affair with Jenkins years ago, an affair that ended when Jenkins moved to the city where I now live.

"No, really, I thought about going on for my doctorate," Gretchen continues. "But I just couldn't stand to see all those books die before my eyes."

"The thing about teaching," I say, "and I'm ashamed to admit it, is the control. It may be an illusion, but for a few hours you feel you have some control."

Gretchen brakes suddenly. "Oh my God," she says and cranes her neck to look up through the windshield.

A double-sized billboard covers nearly the entire outer wall of an old warehouse. Jagged black arrows, labeled "Adultery," "Food Additives," "Abortion," "Euthanasia," and "Teen Suicide" pierce a large glowing Bible. "Shield Yourself From Sin," the caption says. "Read the Bible."

I find a garbage can lid, then climb on top of Gretchen's car and hold the lid like a shield over my breast. "Joan of Arc for the 1980's," I say. Gretchen frames me against the billboard.

"English teachers meet their evil foes," Gretchen adds.

"Happy," Jeff always says to me. "I just want you to be happy."

"Okay," I say Friday in class. "Let's have it. What does Hawthorne have to say about sin?"

Nothing. A few unrelated giggles, a quick pass of a Sony Walkman under the table. A girlish screech rises from the courtyard outside when a bright yellow tennis ball bounces on the outer window sill.

"Take out a sheet of paper," I say wearily. "Time for a pop quiz."

Angie pulls the Walkman's headphones over her ears and defiantly lets her clogs slip off her feet to make a noise like toppling bricks. "You're just so out of it, Ms. Delancy," Angie claims. "Nobody cares about 'Ethan Brand.' Come off it." She turns up the radio and lays her head on the desk.

"Number one," I say to the hushed class. I am shredding hall passes in my fist. "How does Ethan Brand commit the unpardonable sin?"

I slide into a student desk in Gretchen's room. "Is it Happy Hour yet?" I ask. She laughs and shakes chalk dust out of her blazer.

At Mr. J's we order Margaritas, then Mexican Flags and Stingers.

"I'm just not cut out to be a Ms. Delancy," I say, slumping against the bar rail. I tell Gretchen about Angie's outburst, the pop quiz. "Do you think I did the right thing?" I ask. I light a match, then touch it to a book of matches and watch the green flame. "Just what do I want from these kids anyway? For them to remember their notebooks and sit quietly in class everyday?"

"Nope," Gretchen says. "But that's what it comes down to."

"It's not that I don't like what I'm teaching. Hawthorne, Melville, good, evil, fidelity, honor. I love those old words." My cheeks and hands are flushed — I think I have come upon a fundamental truth about myself. I look feverish in the mirror behind the bar. "What am I going to do when we come to the moderns, where everyone's neurotic and forgiveable?"

"Sounds like a good paper topic," Gretchen says. She orders

a round of Brandy Alexanders and we stare into our frothy drinks.

"I'm still living four hundred miles from here," I claim, and shrug off my jean jacket. "Sometimes I wake up fully expecting to walk to campus, not drive to work. I don't even own any work clothes. The attendance secretary still asks to see my hall pass."

"Time to go shopping," Gretchen says, then smiles and laughs. She obviously loves teaching — her skin and eyes are clear, and she is already planning field trips for next year.

"I wish I could embrace my classes the way you do. Maybe I could use some of your discussion sheets," I say.

"Be true to yourself," Gretchen counsels. She reads the drink menu. "Do you want to try a Melon Hummer? We could ask for two straws." I reset my chin on the slick bartop. At six-thirty we go home and I fall asleep until the morning.

Gretchen wheels around the deserted bank parking lot and pulls up next to a large concrete planter filled with flowers. I dash out and yank two geraniums by the roots and place them in a bag on the back seat. Then I go back for two more, taking care not to snap off the blossoms.

"Those are just right," Gretchen says, and pulls out into the road. "We'll hit the savings and loan for impatiens, then scrounge around that construction site for bricks."

I turn up the cassette player in my lap and sing along with David Bowie. We are fixing up our apartment this weekend.

"Is this the way two English teachers should be behaving?" I wonder.

"This *is* the way two English teachers are behaving," Gretchen counters.

We turn down the main suburban shopping street. Huge tempera-paint murals of Trojans skewering rams decorate the store windows; it must be homecoming at the public school.

"Do you ever feel you are living someone else's life?" I ask loudly.

I am holding the phone in the kitchen next to the sink. Mrs. Landon calls me "Miss Delany." "Who chose that book," she demands. "I don't want my Peggy reading it." Peggy Landon is the only black student in my eleventh grade class. The book her mother is referring to is *Huckleberry Finn.*

"You don't know," she claims. "Nigger Jim."

"We're not going to read *Huck Finn* until January," I explain. "We'll talk more about blacks in literature before then."

"I'm pulling her out of that school," she warns. "I'm pulling her right out. What are you trying to do anyway, spreading these lies?"

"I'm just trying to do what I think is right, Mrs. Landon," I say soothingly, but she has hung up.

"I'm going to call Jenkins," I call out to Gretchen.

"And I'm going back to college," Gretchen retorts.

Jeff calls. "I can't make it on the 21st," he says. We have been planning a rendezvous in Chicago during an upcoming long weekend.

"Aw, Jeff," I complain. "That's the only time we can get together until Thanksgiving."

"Right. See you then."

"Who was that?" Gretchen says, opening the refrigerator door.

"I don't know," I say.

I call my mother. "I'm depressed," I moan. "I just can't seem to make myself feel at home."

"You can always leave, honey," my mother reminds me. She usually provides practical, if extreme, counsel.

"True, true," I say. "But then what?"

"Things could come together any day now," she reassures me.

Gretchen and I go to see a movie that night, leaving piles of compositions on the kitchen table.

I see a dark-haired man in army fatigues and a polo shirt talking on the phone.

"Gretchen," I say, and stop in my tracks. "I think I'm in love."

She looks at the man on the phone. "He's fifteen, Marie. Sixteen at the most."

I look more closely. "You're right," I say. "What's happening to me?"

"Better call Jenkins," she advises.

I get roped into chaperoning the sophomore dance. "Oh, please,

Ms. Delancy," the class president begs me. "We want all the young teachers there." Still, Gretchen somehow says no.

Doug Vann, the assistant headmaster, discusses my duties ahead of time. "If you smell anything like alcohol, send them my way. Don't bust anybody on your own."

"Right," I agree. I know I could never bust anyone. I don't have the confidence of my own perceptions. A lot of perfume smells amazingly like alcohol.

I arrive at the dance early; no one is even near the dance floor and all the girls are in the bathroom. Most of my students snub me. They are still miffed that I gave them a long reading and writing assignment over the weekend.

A laughing crowd of seniors bursts into the dark gym. Each one is wearing a baseball cap mounted with a stuffed felt unicorn horn.

"What's going on," I ask Eva Garcia, the second year Spanish teacher.

"Team symbol," she explains. "They're the Knights." The DJ turns up "Don't You Want Me" by Human League and nearly everyone spins out onto the floor.

One of the parent chaperones mistakes me for a student. "Go on out and dance, dear," she urges me. "Looks like Charlie wants to dance."

I sit down and chew on the ice cubes in my punch. I could be Katherine Hepburn, I think. Or Amelia Earhardt. Or Annie Oakley.

I recognize the next song by Boy George and I swing my feet, wishing I had braids. Or an aviator's scarf. Or high cheekbones and trousers.

"Help," I say to Jeff when I finally reach him. "I want out of this place, this job."

"Face it," Jeff replies. "You're a teacher now. You've been teaching since you were in kindergarten."

I hate it that he is right. There is nothing else I could do except read from morning to night.

"So, Thanksgiving," he says.

"Look Jeff, what's happening with Sarah? I don't want to see you if you are still seeing Sarah." I say this very slowly.

21

"Marie," Jeff begins. "Let's just do what we want to do. Be who we are."

"Speak English," I demand, but I know what he means. Jeff is much more than four hundred miles away. I try to remember what Emerson had to say about fidelity — I'd like to impress Jeff with the wrongheadedness of what he is doing. "Well, be happy," I say crisply before I hang up the phone.

I sit for a long time, morosely staring at a bulletin board covered with snapshots of me and Jeff — Jeff bowing in the doorway of my old apartment, Jeff and I on roller skates, Jeff feeding his tropical fish, Jeff and I camping during our first summer together, three years ago. All those days.

I stare at my palms, wondering what might be the right thing to do. Fill up the car with gas and drive four hundred miles? I could seduce Jeff, then lie that I'm pregnant, or weak with a rare heart disease. Call him and nonchalantly say that Jenkins has moved down the block, just to be near me? Sue him? — he owes me nearly a hundred dollars and is causing me mental anguish. Lying, jealousy, greed. There are seven deadly sins. What are the other four?

Finally, I scan the apartment, then begin a flurry of activity. I wash and stack the dishes, straighten up bookshelves, polish the tables, water the plants, light candles. When Gretchen comes home from a meeting, I take her jacket and hang it up. "This is where I live," I explain to her. "Right here. Right here where I am."

INDEPENDENCE DAY

ON MOVING DAY, Lou and I were in the garage sorting through a heap of rusting tools. I found a plastic Cool-Whip container filled with drill bits and tossed it into a cardboard box, then pulled a socket wrench out from under a posthold spade and placed it carefully in a wooden crate. Lou turned on a transistor, swatted at cobwebs with his beefy hand, and set the radio on a window ledge. Spiders scuttled along the cracked wood. Between the trills of static, Lou sang outlaw songs with Wiilie Nelson.

I stood up and wiped my hands on my shorts when I heard gravel crunching on the driveway. I hoped it was my husband, Kenny; Lou and I needed help.

"Hey there," Lou greeted someone familiarly. I continued working when I saw it was Wayne climbing out of his black El Camino. His yellow license plate read, "JOYRIDE Wisconsin." A small American flag drooped from his antenna.

"Hey good lookin'," he waved, and chucked a cigarette butt into a basement window well. He left the car idling to hear Dion sing "Runaway" on the radio. "Hot enough for the fourth of July?" Wayne asked. He produced a sparkler from his shirt pocket, stuck it in the dirt, and lit it with his cigarette lighter. The sparkler sputtered, crackled, then fizzled out. He cheered, flung the hot wire into the bushes, then joined us in the relative cool of the garage.

Leaning in the doorway, Wayne chewed on a farmer's match, and snapped his hands in the air to catch flies in his fist. "Moving day, huh? California, here you come." He shook his fist near his ear and looked up at the rafters. "You're never gonna get this clean without some help. Where's Kenny, old pal o'mine?"

Lou shrugged. "I haven't seen him all morning. He's got quite a bit of packing to do." Lou heaved a hammer head into a box. "Doesn't matter. We can move without him."

I stared at Lou working his jaw muscles, but he only reached for another tool.

Wayne let the fly free to thrum against the window, then asked, "Got plans for that ratchet drill?"

Lou shrugged again and mopped the back of his neck with a red handkerchief. "Probably come in handy. But if you're putting in a bid on it . . . ."

"No, no, no. Just treasure hunting."

Wayne watched me haul a stack of barn wood to the pickup where it landed in the bed with a whomp. He squeezed my biceps admiringly and whistled. "Been working out with Lou's barbells, have you, Margie? We'll have to have us an arm wrestling match here." I rolled my eyes and reached for a broom. "Goin' west, huh? The old pioneer trail," he said, grabbing for another fly.

"West, east, it doesn't matter to me," I said, swiping at the oily dust with my broom. "I just want to get on a road and let it take me somewhere." I peered out the garage door and watched the wind furrow a field of high rye grass. "I'll be glad when I see this town in my rear view mirror."

Wayne followed my gaze. "Got everything you could need right here in Caledonia," he said. "Home of the free. My pop always says, relax, you're in Caledonia."

"Relax?" Lou hooted from behind the lawn mower. "I hope I'm not this relaxed again until I'm six feet under."

Wayne wiped his chin on his T-shirt sleeve. "You two shouldn't be working today anyway. It's a holiday. Got any beer?"

"Check the fridge," I said, glad to send Wayne on an errand. On his way into the house he stopped to turn up the volume on the car radio. Kenny Rogers' voice boomed across the yard, and I wondered again where my husband might be.

When Lou and I finished loading nearly everything from the garage, it was late afternoon. I could feel blisters swelling on my feet, and a fresh rash of sweat beading on my upper lip. Lou turned on a hose, took a long drink, then plunged his head into the cold streaming water. I unlaced my tennis shoes and washed my toes in the puddles he made, then gulped down some water for myself.

Wayne let the screen door bang behind him, then grabbed the hose and threatened to douse me. I turned away, went into the empty kitchen, and brought out three cans of beer to Wayne and Lou squatting on the concrete steps. Wayne popped open his can, licked at the foam, and asked, "Where does Kenny get off having such a good-looking wife," He poked Lou in the stomach. "Huh, Lou?"

Lou smiled and squeezed the beer can until it dented.

"If I were Kenny, I'd keep an eye on her," Wayne said with his eyes on me, "now that you're gonna be roommates."

"Business partners, Wayne, not roommates." Lou rolled his beer can across his forehead.

"Business partners, huh?" Wayne nudged me. "What do you think about this business?"

"This business is our ticket out of here," I replied and stared at a large wasp-shaped birthmark on his neck. It made him look perpetually sunburned. "Kenny always said it was a matter of time and money before we got out of here. Guess he knew we'd get a windfall sooner or later."

Wayne unbuttoned the cuffs around his wrists and rolled his sleeves up his skinny pale arms. He picked at bindweeds growing close to the steps and clogged an anthill with their stems.

"So, you got it all planned out how you're gonna spend your 'windfall' yet?" He scraped a chokeberry branch along the sidewalk, then tested its hot sharpened tip on my toe. My foot twitched away. "How come you never told us 'bout this inheritance coming? Kenny can't keep a secret to shine his shoes."

"Wasn't a secret." Lou swilled his beer and wiped his mouth on his faded T-shirt collar. "Del always said he'd leave this house to me and my brother. Otherwise, he wouldn't have moved up north to Door County. You know that. All of Caledonia knows that."

"When's Mr. Inheritance showing up?" Wayne asked.

"Hell if I know," Lou said, flushing in his sudden anger. "Me and Margie cleared that garage ourselves. Most of it's his junk anyway. We don't need cans of old nails out in California." Lou spat a midge out of his mouth, and pitched his beer can toward a pile of rubbish.

Just then I saw Kenny weaving down the street on his skateboard, looking younger than his twenty-eight years. Red, white and blue streamers attached to his elbows and knees rippled in his wind. He clutched a paper bag under a nut-brown arm and circled on the asphalt in front of us, a patriotic spectacle. Drawing two oranges out of the bag, and puffing out his cheeks, he managed to juggle the oranges and loop into the driveway, gravel sputtering.

Kenny bowed, then crashed into a stained boxspring and lay

sprawling near the trash. He slowly slipped a hand down his right boot, pulled out a flat bottle, and raised it to his mouth. I ran to him, rehearsing angry words, and trampled his tangled streamers on the crushed quartz. He grinned up at me and sent a spurt of amber whiskey into the summer sky. Then he reached into his left boot and pulled out a thick wad of hundred dollar bills. "Five thousand smackeroos. And more where they came from." He ruffled the money in my face, then replaced it in his boot.

I sighed noisily and helped Lou pull him up. Lou said, "You're drunk," spat over Kenny's shoulder, then turned on the hose to shower him with cold water. Kenny lept up to do jumping jacks in his leather boots and cutoffs, then solemnly saluted Lou when he turned the water off with a squeal. Wayne, standing on the driveway with his hands in his back pockets, laughed and stamped his bare feet on the stones. Then he leaned back and whistled with two fingers between his teeth. Lou threw down the hose and stalked into the house.

"Kenny," I said, feeling light-headed, "the show's over."

"You're wrong there, my little chickadee. The show must go on." Kenny pinched my cheek, shook water out of his hair, then inspected the boxes in the pick-up. "Well, sir," he said and whistled. "Looks like you and Lou have been packing all morning." He patted my back pocket, tugged out a book of matches, then squatted on the driveway and lit a small grey pellet. Long papery snakes spiralled out on the stones, shivered, then disintegrated into ash.

"Kenny, please," I said.

"Now don't you start." Kenny winked. "No fussin' on the fourth of July. Says so in the Constitution."

I carried a lamp and some flower pots from the porch to the truck. "The Gallaghers are gonna be here from Racine in a couple hours," I said to Kenny over my shoulder. "You better get your stuff in the truck or we'll have to pay for a motel room."

Wayne slumped out of the garage with a transistor and lit a cigarette for me. Jimmy Buffett sang about wasting away in Margaritaville. Kenny whistled along, circling the truck, then snapped his fingers and said, "That's the ticket. I'll go mix up a pitcher of Margaritas. The all-American drink. Do we have any limes?" He whirled around on the heel of his boot and almost ran

26

into the house.

"Kitchen's empty," I called. I swatted at a cloud of mosquitoes, then slapped Wayne's hand off my hip. "C'mon, Wayne," I whined, backing away from him. I tucked a hank of hair behind my ear. "Let's give Lou a hand in the basement."

Downstairs Lou was stacking two-by-fours and brushing sawdust off his arms. Through the floorboards, we heard Kenny strumming his guitar. He sang "My Tennessee Mountain Home" and "Cold Cold Heart."

Lou pulled me over to the washing machine rumbling with a load of rags and beach towels. "Can't you do something about him, kid? Sweet talk him or bitch him or something?" Lou's clenched hands were white on the washing machine. "He doesn't listen to me anymore. You're his wife." He opened his hands in supplication.

I shrugged and backed away. "He doesn't listen to me either. You tell me the right words, and I'll say them."

Lou circled a drain set in the concrete. "I know he's cooking up something. What's he doin' with all that cash?"

"Listen, Kenny knows what he's doing."

'Sure he knows what he's doing — keeping us from going to California."

"Wait a minute. We can make lots of money in California. Why would Kenny want to stay?" I chewed on a loose curl hanging below my ear. I had the same doubts when I saw the flask in Kenny's boot.

"He's foolin' around, Margie. He's being cagey. Cagey, you know what I mean? I've seen him do foolish, desperate things. I've seen him."

I rubbed my eyes, suddenly fatigued. "Yeah, well I'm leaving for California tonight by hook or by crook." Lou arched his eyebrows. For a moment in the dim cellar light, Lou looked like Andy Griffith. "But I'd rather go with Kenny. He's my husband, and we should all go together. It ought to be that way."

Lou's T-shirt was dark green with sweat. He shook his head at me, and, hearing Kenny launch into "Behind Closed Doors," ran up the stairs in three clumsy bounds. I followed quickly, knowing Lou could do something ugly, and found him in the front room, standing over Kenny and scowling.

"Put down that stupid guitar and start packing." Lou clenched and unclenched a nail in his fist. "How come I'm doing all the work around here? It's your house."

Kenny was sitting on the bare floor, leaning back against the white wall. It made his irises seem unnaturally blue. He was surrounded by gold cups and framed parchments: his bowling, softball and old high school trophies.

"Our house, Lou," Kenny said, fingering chords on the frets of his guitar. "You've been right brotherly to let Margie and me live here, but it's always been your home away from home. Aren't you gonna miss this place?"

Lou slipped the nail into his pocket and ran his hand through his thinning hair. Kenny picked some guitar chords. Lou and I sat down and crossed our legs Indian-style. I had seen Kenny like this before; it was best to wait and let him make the first move. Otherwise, he was prone to do something dramatic, violent even.

Wayne peeked into the room, then strolled in, beer cans and a bag of peanuts in his arms. "Looks like the new owners are late," Wayne said, winking at me. Kenny gulped Jack Daniels from his flask. We could hear the thump and brass of a parade a few blocks away.

"Sing a song about California," Wayne demanded, cracking open some nuts. He threw some peanuts into the air and caught one in his mouth.

"Nope, no songs about California. I don't even want to think about California." Kenny nudged his guitar to the floor where it landed with a discordant, hollow clatter. He stood up and stretched out his arms. "What's so great about California? We got everything anybody could want right here in Wisconsin." He winked at me, stomping his boots on the wooden floor. "And now we've even got our own house. Never thought I'd own my own home at twenty-eight." Outside there was a boom and a whee of fireworks already starting.

"You're talking trash, Kenny." Lou got to his feet. "It was your idea to move west in the first place. You were talking about it at Del's funeral."

Kenny smashed a silverfish with his toe and turned around to look out the window. Over the hollyhock vines, I could see the eastern sky fade and darken. "I've been checking around, Lou. Ran into Frazier, you know, from the Department of Transportation. He mentioned, over a couple of drinks, of course, that they were planning to run a new highway along here, the exit ramp right at our doorstep."

Kenny turned, face red with a smile. "Then it hit me, bright as day. Got our future in my pocket." Kenny patted his hip pocket, then swigged from the bottle at his feet. "We should thank our lucky stars that we just happen to have the capital for the right kind of investment. Thanks to Del, of course. We can call it 'Del's Goldmine' or maybe just 'Del's Place.'"

"What are you talking about," Lou demanded. "Call what 'Del's Place?'"

"The new roadside restaurant we're gonna open up. Right here. We can all three live upstairs, work down here and watch the money pour in with every cup of coffee. Frazier assured me it would be a major truck route. Truckers drink gallons of coffee. Why, we'll get rich on java alone."

Kenny patted Lou on the back. "And the beauty of it is, we don't have to go anywhere. Why go to California to get rich, when we can stay right here and count our money?"

I glared at Kenny and said, "Kenny, California is more than money." Wayne snickered and slapped his knee.

We all stared at the window when we heard someone pull into the driveway. "Well, it's too late to change your mind. The new owners are here now." Lou turned to Kenny triumphantly. "Pack up your guitar."

Instead, Kenny ran outside and greeted the Gallaghers as they jumped down out of their van. Lou and I watched him from the window. Roman candles and fizgigs burst and sparkled above their heads. Mr. Gallagher scratched his chest, squinted up at the house, and looked down at something Kenny had in his hand. Kenny nodded vigorously, jerked his thumb toward the house, then toward the pick-up. When Kenny reached into his boot and pulled out his roll of bills, Lou and I ran out the door. Wayne moved to the windows to watch.

"Hello, Mister, Mrs. Gallagher," Lou said, shaking hands. "What's going on here?"

Mr. Gallagher pushed his baseball hat off his forehead, looked at the money in Kenny's hand, and said, "Well."

I smiled at Mrs. Gallagher, and leaned against the slatted fence. She had her dark hair tied back with a striped ribbon, and wore a pink cotton shirtwaist and straw sandals. I felt sooty and rumpled, and longed to take a shower. Mr. Gallagher began again. "Well, it seems, Mr. Dobbs, your brother here, changed his mind about selling the place. Seems he's willing to give us back the thirty thousand we already paid for it, plus five thousand for our troubles if we drop the whole deal."

"Exactly right, Mr. Gallagher. You are a sharp cookie." Kenny began to count the bills.

"Wait a minute, wait a minute," Lou said, bumping Kenny's elbow. "You can't just do that, pay these people off. They want this house."

Mrs. Gallagher watched the hundred dollar bills flutter in Kenny's hand. "We'd better talk this over, Bill," she said. Mr. Gallagher walked over to the van, leaned against the front fender, and scratched his chest. He nodded as he listened to his wife talk. She climbed into the front seat, then Mr. Gallagher strode toward us. "Sounds like a fine deal, sir," he said, shaking Kenny's hand again.

"But there are papers and everything," I said weakly.

"We can take care of that tomorrow. Today's a legal holiday anyway." Kenny finished counting the money and ceremoniously handed it to Mr. Gallagher.

My arm twitched; I wanted to bat the money away, slap Kenny and prevent him from shaking Mr. Gallagher's hand. Already I could see Kenny's bewildered face collapsing into anger, my victorious shrug. But I felt a familiar burning helplessness and self-loathing; I wouldn't act to stop Kenny. He had it all planned, staged even. I stepped into his blocked-out scenes, as I had before, because this was our dance: he was the con and I was the sucker.

Lou jumped into the back of his pick-up and started throwing what belonged to Kenny out on the lawn. "You won't get away with this, Kenny. Seems you forgot the house is half mine." His voice was high and strained. "I could take you to court." Boxes of dishes and cans of nails crashed on the grass.

I sat on the porch railing, swinging my legs until the Gallaghers tooted and drove off. Kenny would just buy Lou out. He'd probably planned to all along, rake in that thirsty truckers' money for himself. Kenny went in for his guitar, and Wayne trailed out after him.

Wayne pinched my butt and said, "No one leaves for California without some kind of showdown." Out over the tops of trees, I could see spots of light wriggle into the early evening sky with a thin whistle, then explode into starbursts and trickle down into the trees.

Wayne looked out over the treetops. "Wild, aren't they? Fireworks were always my favorite part of the fourth of July." Wayne watched the explosions reflected on my face. "Watcha gonna do now, Margie?"

"It would be really terrific, Wayne, if you could just leave me alone and give me some time to think. All right?" I looked at Kenny turning his guitar. Wayne slipped off the railing and strolled down the walk.

"Kenny," I said, my lips tight around a cigarette filter, "so what's the secret?"

Kenny sipped whiskey from a cardboard cup printed with American flags. "The secret is, babe," he said, focusing on the red glow of my cigarette tip, "that there is no secret. Everything is the same as it was before. Except that now we have a bit more loot to play with, and a profitable future staring us in the face." He strummed something unfamiliar. "Time to lay down some roots, as they say. Have a baby."

"Kenny," I said, squinting at the sky, "I don't want to even think about having a baby right now. I want to get in that truck and go."

" 'Course you want to have a baby." He nuzzled my ear. "Check your BC lately?" BC was our code name for diaphragm. My head felt light, as if it were floating to the stars. I saw that Kenny's smile — crooked and ingenuous — was the same smile that had pulled me here to him four summers back. I understood our last year of trouble had come down to this: I wanted to go, but Kenny could make me stay.

As the sharp retort of a backyard firecracker echoed, Lou marched up the porch and yanked me down off the railing. "C'mon,

Margie. Give me a hand."

Lou pulled me to the truck. He picked up a box of hammers, hatchets, and small saws and dumped them on the lawn. I said, "Suddenly, Lou, I feel very tired, old even."

Wayne laughed. "Looks like this happy threesome is going to split up." He sauntered over to the truck and put his arm around me, saying, "I think you two should go out to California and Margie can stay here with me." He kissed my cheek and I wiggled out of his sweaty grasp. Flares squibbed and twinkled like fireflies in the western sky.

Lou climbed into the pick-up, started the engine and turned on his headlights, illuminating Kenny's rubbled belongings. I scanned the too-familiar street, the slatted fence. I wanted to be on a highway, not hear it outside my window. I kissed Kenny quickly, then joined Lou in the front seat.

"Margie," Kenny bellowed. "You can't go." He lit a cherry bomb and threw it in front of the truck.

"We'll send you an address if you change your mind," Lou yelled to Kenny, then turned to me. "You all set?" I nodded. I had been ready to leave all year. I looked down at my stomach. Once we got to California, I could take things one day at a time. Call Kenny and try again. Lou released the hand brakes with a whir.

Kenny circled around the truck and leaned into my window. "You don't want to go. California stinks. It's sinking."

I touched his cheek and whispered, "It's not too late. Climb in. Let's get out of here until our heads are clear. Start fresh."

Kenny wheeled away, then banged the fender with his fist. "You can't go, Margie. Don't you want to raise our family right here in our hometown?"

I picked at the fray of my cutoffs. "It's not my hometown, Kenny," I said quietly.

Wayne crouched in front of the truck and arranged a circle of sparklers and firecrackers around an American flag propped in the gravel. He lit the fuses, and stood at attention. "A twelve-gun farewell salute," he said. He hopped around the sparklers as the firecrackers began to pop.

Lou backed the truck down the driveway, then braked.

"Don't go," Kenny warned. He scrambled out on the lawn,

picked up a hatchet, and sprinted down the driveway. He stood in the headlights and raised the hatchet above his shoulder. Lou pulled on the parking brake. A serpent of green light snaked above Kenny's head, then burst into a pinwheel with a sizzle and a bang. Kenny brought the hatchet down on the headlight, but it caroomed off the glass and gashed his thigh.

I screamed and shuddered, watched him crumple, then jumped out of the truck and ran to him. It was hard to tell at first if he seriously hurt himself, but a small circle of blood on his leg, dark as ink, widened as Kenny bent to look at it.

Lou cursed, then followed me out of the cab and ran to him. I reached Kenny first, my pulse beating like small explosions, and stood over him a moment before stooping to check his wound. It would be just like Kenny to fake this whole thing, use a rubber-bladed hatchet and a plastic bag of ketchup. But when I wiped the blood away and saw a flap of skin, I realized his drama was a sign: he'd never let me go.

Kenny pulled his Jack Daniels bottle out of his boot, gulped, and sent a spray of amber whiskey into the dark summer sky. "Don't go," he repeated. I could see that he was trembling, frightened by the loss of real blood.

Lou swore softly, then ripped his green T-shirt, fixed a rough bandage on his brother's bleeding leg, and swatted the flies from the wound. We carried Kenny over to Wayne's El Camino. I arranged blankets and pillows in the back, then we lifted Kenny in. "I'll wait here," I said. I didn't feel like going anywhere anymore.

Kenny started to sing "Up Against the Wall, Redneck Mother," and improvised the words. Lou clambered in the back with him while Wayne drove to the hospital. I waved them off, then began to unload the pick-up, singing cheating songs with Tammy Wynette on the radio. Then I took a bath and called the hospital. Kenny was stitched up and ready to come home. When the last fireworks whizzed and exploded, and red, white, and blue skyrockets lit up the sky, I saw the El Camino pull into the driveway, and I toasted Independence Day with a fresh can of beer.

BIRTHDAY

IT IS HEATHER'S BIRTHDAY. Joe wakes the boys early, and they drive through a cold drizzle to the bakery to buy a cake, frosted white as chalk.

Heather stands at the bedroom window in a bathrobe, watching her station wagon, its wiper flapping, pull into the driveway. Three doors open, then her sons and husband fall out. They move jerkily, like toys, toward the house. Justin long-jumps over a ditch, then runs across the wet lawn, blue hood bobbing. Jason follows, hands out front like a tackle, chuffing and slipping up the porch. Heather hears the rattle and thump of the door below, then Joe yells, his words a frozen fog, and Justin darts out of the garage to retrieve something woolen — a hat? mittens? — from the back seat. As Joe carries a white box up the drive and out of her sight, Heather unexpectedly remembers the year she worked late most nights and Joe stayed home with the boys. Did he watch her arrive then?

Heather finds the boys playing transportation lotto at the kitchen table. Birthday presents Heather opened the day before, when her mother visited, are stacked on the extra chair. Sometimes the rooms in her house surprise her with their brightness: they look like they are about to be filmed. Heather dims the kitchen light.

"Hey guys," Heather says, reaching for the coffeepot. "Where's Dad?" she asks, hearing the clink of dumbbell weights in the garage.

Justin stands to scoop strawberry jam on his muffin. "Garage," he reports, cramming a full slice in his mouth. A red blob of jam plops on his rugby shirt, and Heather frowns. Justin looks down, then shrugs, a gesture Heather has not witnessed before.

She sits, hands clutching the coffee mug. She has never been one to brood over birthdays, but now she is thinking of years, of aging.

"Jason," she says, and smiles when he buzzes his lips, practicing his sound effects. She is still surprised sometimes by Jason's face; he looks much like Joe did when she first met him. Joe's face doesn't look like that now — open and amazed; it has darkened and folded

34

over the years. Heather forgets what she wanted to say to Jason, and reflexively points to his napkin when he looks up.

Joe stands in the doorway wearing golf gloves and squinting into a Nikon set on a tripod. When he lowers the camera, Heather sees that she is right: Joe looks flushed and jowly.

"What time is her plane?" Joe asks, scowling at the light meter.

"Later. Four-fifteen." Heather watches Joe's hands. "Ah, what's with the gloves, Joe? You golfing in the sleet or what?"

Joe clenches and unclenches his fists. "Nope. I'm just thinking about golfing. Maybe I'll take the boys to a golf movie round about four-fifteen. What do you say, guys?"

Both boys look up expectantly. Then Justin narrows his eyes. "A *golf* movie? he asks, thrusting forward his hip. "What kind of golf movie?"

Heather stands to wipe an already-cleaned counter. "Why can't you just relax and practice being civil to Sue? It's not so hard. She'll be here a week, and you can't be off at a movie the whole time. Why do you have to make things so complicated? It would all be so much simpler if you could just relax and stay calm." As if to demonstrate, Heather calmly rinses the sponge to wipe the counter again.

"It just doesn't work," Joe explains. "We never get along. She has one drink, and it's curtains. She gets serious and starts asking me questions. Am I happy? Do I like being a father? Jeez. She doesn't quit."

Joe points the camera at Heather to focus it. Heather can see herself reflected upside down inside the lens, hair flat against her head like a cap. The camera looks like a toy in Joe's fleshy palms.

"C'mon guys," Joe says. "What do you say? 'Raiders' is playing at the Villa for ninety-nine cents. We'll go when I finish this roll."

Heather feels weightless, airborne. She hears a click and a whir as Joe approaches with the camera.

"C'mon, honey," Joe says. "Do I have to say cheese? It's your birthday."

Heather crosses her hands in front of her face. "Turn that thing off. I'm not even dressed yet."

Joe points the camera at the boys, frames them as they begin to laugh and sing "Happy Birthday." Joe crouches and shoots. "Go get dressed, honey," he says, winding the film.

"Yeah, go get dressed, Mom," Jason chides.

"I want to get you in here too," Joe says. He is snapping pictures as he speaks. "You'll regret it years from now if I don't."

Heather squeezes her leather gloves and paces, watching a plane sink through a haze like cigar smoke and taxi up to the gate. When Sue emerges into the waiting area, Heather first notices the unwashed hair loosely curled under her beret, then the thinness of her face and the light, purplish puffiness around her eyes. Heather's forehead puckers with an involuntary frown. As they hug, Sue pats Heather's back and says, "I'm so tired. Flying saps my energy and makes me feel old. I must look old and terrible. The gimlets didn't help any either." Sue steps back and rubs the corner of her eyes, then flutters her hands like leaves in front of her face.

"You can take a hot shower at my place," Heather says, silently phrasing questions for later. She reaches for Sue's bag, and guides her down the hall.

"How's Joe?" Sue asks. To her right, planes float to the tarmac outside the window.

Heather smiles at the sight of Sue framed by the mullions, and is reminded of Joe's photographs. "Oh," she begins. "He's big on photography and weight lifting now. He's got Kodak paper and barbells all over the house." They turn up the hall and follow a tall man carrying a poodle in a plastic crate slit with airholes.

"Do you have a cigarette?" Sue asks. "I need a cigarette."

Heather pulls a crushed pack of Carletons from her purse, and shakes one out for Sue.

Sue points to the crated poodle, who stares back with eyes black and glassy as marbles, then yaps and bares its teeth. Sue elbows Heather, then sticks her thumbs in her ears, trills her tongue, and waggles her fingers. The poodle lunges, its claws clicking against the plastic, and yaps. Sue winks at its owner when he looks back over his shoulder.

"Sue," Heather says. "The cigarette."

"Hold on," Sue says, index finger wagging. She approaches a cart with a striped awning where a woman is selling flowers from big white tubs. The woman twists thin green paper around the stems of blue carnations, and hands them to a pair of teenage girls.

Still holding the pack of cigarettes in her outstretched hand, Heather stands close enough to the flower cart to smell the fresh, washed scent of the flowers and the fruity muskiness of Sue's perfume.

"Look at these roses, Heather," Sue says without turning her head. "I love roses when they're the color of peaches."

The man with the poodle stops to buy a newspaper, then weaves through the crowd past Heather and Sue.

The flower vendor makes a cone out of white paper to wrap the roses Sue selects. Sue takes the bouquet, rummages in her purse, then snaps open her jaw. "Oh, wow," Sue exclaims, and points over the top of Heather's head. "That guy just stole my dog." She runs down the hall, flowers in hand, high heels clicking on the airport linoleum.

Heather watches the flower vendor, cheeks bright and wind-chapped, eyes pale as stones, chase Sue. She catches up to Sue at a video game, where Sue grins, then opens her purse and hands the vendor some bills.

When Heather meets up with Sue, someone is playing the video game, flashy and loud as a carnival. Sue unwraps the flowers and absent-mindedly presents Heather a dusty-orange rose. "Sue," Heather begins. "What was that all about?" Seven days with Sue now loom as hectic and tiring.

Sue walks away toward the baggage area. "Why can't people just laugh a few things off?" she asks quietly. "Is that too much to ask?" She plops a rose bud down into an ashtray filled with white sand, fine as salt.

In the parking ramp, Sue covers her nose and mouth with a silk scarf and coughs. "The fumes, Heather! How can you breathe these fumes?"

Heather wraps an arm around Sue's shoulders and feels inappropriately maternal. She thinks momentarily of Joe and the boys at the movies, and longs to be home. "Let's get you home," she says firmly.

"Oh, the hell with the shower," Sue cries gaily. Her voice reverberates off of the rows of parked cars. "I have an absolute craving for a White Russian. Let's go straight to Dusty's."

Heather smiles, too wide, giving in. "You're the boss."

As Heather drives, Sue chatters, one topic triggering another: her ex-husband, the secret power of the NRA, the malls in Minneapolis, the death of her cat, the flirtatious young men at the store she manages.

Heather smiles playfully. "Hold it, hold it," she says. "Let's get specific here." She cocks her head, and mumbles conspiratorially, "Any possibilities?"

Sue hoots. "Oh, c'mon. They're youngsters." She crosses her ankles primly. "Besides, this time around I want someone older. Mellowed. You know what I mean? Of course, all those men are married." She turns suddenly to look at the sky, gray as ice. "Married men are good for affairs only anyway. The last affair I had with a married man was too frustrating. After a couple of weeks, he told me I was impossible." Sue snorts. "Can you beat that? Impossible."

Heather pulls into a parking lot and pinches the bridge of her nose. She feels the dull thud of blood in her ears.

Sipping their drinks in the restaurant, Sue keeps talking, seemingly cheered by her litany. Heather listens, sips and nods, watching Sue's hands pat and smooth her cocktail napkin.

"Listen, I'm starving," Heather says, flipping open her menu. "You must be hungry too. Let's order."

Sue's face sags. She clinks a fingernail against her highball glass. "Oh, go ahead, eat, Heather. I don't want anything."

Heather looks up and frowns. "Something wrong, Sue?" she asks, relieved to utter the words she has been rehearsing.

Sue's mouth crumples. "Thirty-three years, Heather," she says wearily, her voice like sand. "I've been eating for thirty-three years, day after day, and I'm just sick of it. Sick of it." She rests her forehead on the corner of the table and sighs, low and keening.

Heather awkwardly reaches over the candles and table settings between them to rub the top of Sue's head.

"It's sad, Heather," she says into her lap. When she looks up, her wet eyes are round and beautiful in the candlelight. "I'm just so tired is all," she claims, and scrapes a cocktail stirrer along the placemat, leaving thickening spirals on the paper.

Heather and Sue arrive home late, a floodlamp illuminating

the front lawn lacy with rime. They exaggerate their steps up the driveway and snicker when Heather pats her pockets for her house keys. She finally rings the doorbell. Sue peers in a side window. "Here comes Joe," she stage-whispers. "He looks so avuncular."

Both gasp and laugh loudly, and when Joe opens the door, he stands for a moment, blinking at the night and the two women, their shoulders slumped and shaking. Joe scratches the side of his nose, then holds open the storm door, smiling stiffly at Sue in case she greets him.

Joe's friends, Bruce and Danny, are sitting at the kitchen table holding fans of playing cards. Sue has already usurped Joe's chair and is munching peanuts, asking Bruce, a spokesman for Amtrak, how train schedules are determined. Danny gets up to pop open four bottles of beer.

"Gin rummy?" Heather asks, and sits down to watch Joe rearrange the cards in his hand. He flexes his biceps nervously. She wonders what he meant by a golf movie. A movie about golf? A movie as long as eighteen holes?

Sue picks up the stack of cards in the middle of the table and shuffles them out in front of Joe, making a rough rectangle.

"A gypsy among us," Danny says, and makes abracadabra motions with his hands.

"Pick a card," Sue says to Joe, who grimaces at Heather. "C'mon, Joe. It's all in the cards."

Joe's neck is ropy and red; he crushes a pile of peanut shells and sifts them onto the table top.

"I think Joe is supposed to shuffle them." Heather slips off her shoes and yawns. "Isn't that right?"

"It's too late now, anyway," Bruce says. "She's supposed to be using tarot cards."

"No, these cards are just fine," Sue says. "They speak to me." She scans the table. Everyone arranges their faces into neutral expressions. Heather realizes Sue has had too much to drink; she could say anything. Heather catches Joe's eye and smiles helplessly, but he sets his jaw and swirls the ice cubes in his club soda.

Sue riffles the cards in her hands. "Danny," she says. "You look like a married man. How's it going?" She whispers, sounding throaty and intimate. "I mean, do you like being married?"

39

"You don't have to answer that," Joe says, glaring at Sue. "In fact, don't answer that."

"No, no, it's okay," Danny claims. He looks at his fingernails thoughtfully. "Let's see. The other night Bette, my wife, and I went off to the mall over here on Rinnick Road, just to shop around, you know, get out of the house. And we ended up at this pet shop, see. It's a relief to be telling somebody this. Now Bette has been wanting to have kids for a long time, ever since we were first married five, six years ago. And she was having a hard time in this pet shop. Sometimes that happens. Little things just set her off."

Danny inhales roughly, and wipes the lip of his beer bottle with his thumb. "It was getting to me too, six years of this. So we stayed in that pet store until it closed, picked out a Burmese kitten, a cocker spaniel pup, some kind of colored bird, and an aquarium for the angel fish. All of it was pretty expensive too, what with the outlay of food and equipment and shots at the vet. They got us coming and going. But it might be worth it. You know?" Danny finally swigs some beer. "Pets could help. You never know."

"Christ," Joe says, throwing down the cards. "Anyone want another beer?"

Sue holds a fan of cards in front of Bruce. "Pick a card, any card," she says and winks. "Let's see if there's a big romance in your future. Someone short, blonde, and pretty."

"I think I better get going," Bruce claims, looking out the window at the stars like frost in the sky.

"Shy about the future, are you?" Sue says. Now Heather glares at her, although she knows Sue will not acknowledge this. "All right. We'll skip you and give Joe his turn. Certainly Joe's got something on his mind."

"I think we've all had enough," Heather says slowly.

Joe stands at the breadbox, a can opener and a beer bottle in each hand. "I'll tell you what's on my mind." He jerks a thumb behind him. "The birthday cake in the cupboard here. I just can't get it out of my mind. Neither could the boys, with it just sitting on the counter, the candles all ready to go."

Heather has covered her face with her hand. "Oh, god, Joe," Heather says from behind her fingers. "I forgot about the cake. I can't believe it, but I forgot." Her hand slips down into the bowl of peanuts. "Are you going to crucify me for that?"

The phone rings. Heather wants to let it ring until it stops; answering it promises to complicate things. She waits, then stands to answer it. Handing the receiver to Sue, she explains, "It's Dodge."

Sue stretches the coiled cord out into the hall, and whispers sternly, "Dodge, how did you get this number?"

Danny and Bruce are zipping their jackets. "Who or what is Dodge, to be calling at this hour?" Joe demands loudly.

"Dodge is Sue's ex-husband. You know that." Heather tucks her shoes under her elbow. "I'm going to bed. We can have the cake for breakfast."

"Don't you leave me down here alone with her," Joe hisses.

"Well, come to bed then." Heather yawns. "See Bruce and Danny to the door and come to bed." She starts up the stairs.

Joe grasps the banister and leans close to Heather's face. "She's got me all excited. Can't you see that? I don't know how she did it, but I'm jumpy as hell." His knuckles are white on the ball of the stairpost. "We never even see you when she's around."

Heather is suddenly very sleepy; Joe's face is as fuzzy and insubstantial as if she'd dreamed it. "She's my guest, Joe, so work it out, huh?" Heather rubs her temples slowly. "Work it out or this week will be disastrous." She turns and mounts the stairs. She has climbed these stairs thousands of times, day after day, but tonight each step seems higher than usual, the carpet a peculiar color; she is not sure there has always been a railing on each side of the stairway.

When Heather reaches the second floor, she crouches to see Joe pacing in the hallway. "How many years have we lived here, Joe?" she asks.

Joe rubs his neck. "This house? Twelve years, honey, maybe thirteen."

Twelve years, Heather thinks, and only today I notice how wide these halls are, how bright the lights. We are moths batting around the inside of an enormous lampshade.

Heather sleeps late, dreaming of a house with endless rooms. In the dream, she hears people opening and closing doors as they come and go, but when she turns toward the noise, the room is empty.

At noon, she awakens and finds the kitchen table set with dessert plates. Sue sits on the floor in front of the TV in the family room, playing Scrabble with Justin. Her cheeks are sooty with mascara, and her hair is in pigtails, tied with bright green yarn bows. Jason flips through the dictionary and watches a Three Stooges rerun on the screen.

"Morning," Heather says groggily. She hears the gargle of rain in the gutter. "How long have you been up?"

"Oh, I can't sleep much anymore," Sue claims, reaching for the dictionary. "And these two were in and out all morning before it started raining."

Heather understands the door sounds in her dream.

Sue runs her finger down a column of words. "Hey guys, a word for me. Amorist. You think I look like an amorist?"

"It's your turn," Justin reminds her.

Joe walks in from the garage wearing a thick wool shirt-jacket. "Hunting, eh?" Heather stretches. "Yesterday it was golfing and now it's hunting?"

"I've been shopping," Joe explains. "Got your Oreo ice cream for you, Sue. Let's cut into that cake."

Heather waits until Sue and the boys are in the kitchen, then says to Joe, "Looks like I missed something here this morning."

"Yep," Sue calls from the kitchen. "Joe and I had a little heart-to-heart while you were sleeping in. Didn't we, Joe?"

"Guess so," Joe agrees. He is unpacking a home movie camera. "Set up the lights, will ya, Justin?"

Heather sits at her place and scoops some frosting off the cake with a finger. Seeing a stack of curled photographs on an extra chair, she picks them up to stare at herself. In one picture, Joe shot up through the triangle her crossed arms created, and caught her looking stern and cross. The half-shadows emphasized the planes and rills on her face, making her look old and destitute, as in a Depression photograph. She shuffles it to the bottom, then rolls the whole stack into the pocket of her bathrobe.

"What's a heart-to-heart?" Jason asks.

As Heather begins to answer, she hears an unearthly fluting like something out of a sci-fi movie. Sue is playing a kind of polished wooden flute Heather has never seen before, and its hollow sound is exacerbating the headache she has had since she woke up. When the music stops, Heather turns to see Sue sip an amber liquid out of a cordial glass: Amaretto or Drambuie.

"What did Dodge want last night?" Heather asks.

Sue stands behind her, but Heather can see Sue reflected in the patio doors. "Oh, I don't want to explain that all now. I just told Joe that whole story."

"Well, what was it like? I mean, was everything okay?" Heather asks, surprised that she is pressing the point.

"What was it like? I don't know. Everything is like something else. It doesn't matter, does it? Let's celebrate your birthday."

Sue leaves the room, and Heather hears the closet door, then the front door open and close. Joe begins to light the candles on the cake, which looks dusty in the dips of frosting. "Where's she going?" Heather ask Joe.

"You'll see. Just make a wish." He trains the whining camera on the cake, then on Justin who holds a sign which reads, "March, 1985."

Heather winks at Jason, closes her eyes, but can't think what to wish. She blinks and smiles, then purses her lips to blow. She is surprised to see Sue standing out in the rain on the patio wearing a fur coat. Sue bends and poses like a pin-up girl, then opens the coat to reveal a silver bikini and blows a kiss at Heather, whose lips are still pursed to blow out the candles. Justin and Jason stare out the patio door until Justin asks, "What is she doing out there?" He rolls his eyes.

Joe jerks open the door. "What do you think you're doing?"

Sue's pouty smile fades and she shrugs. "All wrong, huh? This is all wrong?" She clutches the collar of the fur coat. "I only had a couple Drambuies. I forgot about the boys."

"You bet this is all wrong," Joe yells, and yanks her back into the kitchen. Sue's hair is glistening with tiny drops of rain; it looks as if she is wearing a tiara.

Joe's jaw muscles jump inside his cheek. "That's not what you were supposed to do. That's not what we agreed to." Joe is standing so close to Sue that for a moment Heather thinks he could kiss her.

43

Both Justin and Jason watch the candles melt into small pools of wax on the cake.

Heather stands. "Maybe it's just me," she says. "Maybe I'll just leave you two alone again and let you work it out." She pulls a trenchcoat out of the closet and wraps it around her flannel robe, then steps into a pair of rubber shoes. "See you later," she calls.

"Heather, hold it." Joe clears his throat.

"No, really, it's okay. I'll be back later." She walks out the door to her car.

Heather drives around the block a few times, then decides she is hungry, so she follows Maple Street out to where she doesn't recognize the cross-streets, where Maple turns into Highway 12. Everything is grayed and flattened by the rain; what she sees through her windshield might as well be a photograph.

Lured by pink neon, Heather turns into the parking lot of the Silver Dollar Diner. She finds a tube of lipstick in her coat pocket, strokes on some the color of paprika, and fluffs her hair in the rear-view mirror. Feeling something bump against her hip, Heather digs into her pockets and unrolls Joe's photographs. She stares at her old, shadowed face and cannot remember Joe crouching low enough to snap a picture from such a strange angle. Joe's actions and desires seem suddenly alien to her. Why would he develop such a shot?

Heather leafs through the rest of the curled stack, smiling at Justin and Jason hamming it up, until a small yellowed snapshot falls onto her lap. In its borders, two people are pictured at a costume party: a man in a wild paisley-print shirt drunkenly hugging a woman in a polka-dot mini-dress. His lips are pressed to her neck, his hand cupped under her breast. Her pulse beating loudly against her temple, Heather stares hard into their faces; behind the fake mutton-chop sideburns and thick eyeliner and blush, Heather recognizes Joe and Sue. She checks the border date: March, 1983. Turning it over and over, and peering at the faces again, Heather feels she is not Joe's wife, just some stray woman in a diner parking lot who found the photographs blown against a wire wastebasket.

Heather sees that a girl of fourteen or so is watching her from the cab of a pick-up in the parking lot, and Heather quickly slips

44

the photo in the glove compartment. Instead of feeling angry or betrayed, Heather is embarrassed for both Joe and Sue. Joe was drinking in those days too. Heather has already decided she will never mention the photo to either Joe or Sue; after all, she thinks, 1983 was two years ago. When she gets out of the car, she hears a familiar voice — Kenny Rogers or Willie Nelson — leaking out of the truck.

In the diner, everything on the menu sounds good. Heather orders walnut pancakes, specialty of the house, and scrambled eggs, Canadian bacon, toast and coffee. She eats slowly, concentrating on cutting and chewing, then washes her hands in the employee bathroom and considers ordering another cup of coffee.

When she returns to the counter, an older man in a bowling jacket is sitting on Heather's stool. He sees her frowning at him in the mirror. "You comin' or goin', honey?"

Heather is momentarily stumped. "Well, neither, I guess. I just wanted a second cup of coffee." Heather sits a couple stools away from the man, dissatisfied with her explanation.

"Miss," he says, cocking his finger at the waitress. "Get the lady another cup of coffee."

Heather thinks the man looks like an older version of Al Pacino, or a caricature of a cab driver. He wears the same kind of soft cotton shirt as Joe, with the collar band of his T-shirt peeking out. The waitress sets a fresh cup of coffee and tiny sealed buckets of half and half in front of her.

"You in a hurry?" the man asks, looking at the ruffle of her nightgown slipping out of her coat.

Heather shakes her head and sips.

"Good. Everyone's in too much of a hurry nowadays. You know what I mean?"

Heather tries to think of a reply, but just says, "Well," and laughs dryly, as if she is coughing.

"Yep, just rushing around," the man continues. "They break their necks getting someplace, then kill themselves trying to get back out the door." A steaming plate of food arrives, and he punctures two egg yolks with a corner of toast.

Heather stirs her coffee and nods. "Mmm, I know what you mean."

"Can't blame 'em, though. Gotta be honest about it. We're all worried about coming and going. You know what I mean?" He chomps his rippled bacon, then lists, "High school graduation, leaving for the service, getting married, funerals. Your whole life is just getting to a place, then leaving it, if you want to look at it that way."

Chewing a cuticle, Heather worries vaguely about Jason and Justin. "You're so right," she says.

"It's the little things, too. You look a sharp woman. Maybe you'll understand this." The man leans toward Heather, and suddenly she likes this man, his ethnic face, the rough cadence of his speech, his big hands, yellow in the diner light.

"I'm a happily married man, a family man. Don't like too many surprises. But everytime I get home and walk in the door, I'm a little nervous, excited that maybe this time, something will be different." He leans even closer, his fingers almost touching hers. "Same thing with leaving in the morning."

"Is it ever?" Heather asks. "Different, I mean?"

"Oh, sure. Sometimes everything is completely changed. An outsider could never tell, but you know. You can smell it. It keeps you going."

"I don't know," Heather says, joking now. "Sounds dangerous."

"Oh, it is. Sure it is," the man says with wide Rodney Dangerfield eyes. "But what isn't? Tell me that."

Driving back, Heather feels refreshed, clear-headed for the first time in days, though it is dark and stormy outside. She plans what to do for the rest of Sue's visit to keep her out of Joe's hair: movies, the botanical gardens, an afternoon at a health center. She wonders if she really enjoys Sue anymore, and realizes the man in the diner was right: everything has changed since Sue's arrival.

When she parks in the driveway, Heather notices that the kitchen lights are on. Seized with a playful urge, she tramps into the backyard and heads for the patio. In the darkness of the late afternoon, she feels a bit breathless, as if peeking into her house were some kind of forbidden pleasure.

Standing at the edge of the lawn, she sees the birthday cake, somewhat crooked now, still displayed in the middle of the kitchen table. Sue runs in front of it, face contorted, pigtails shaking. Because of the rain on the patio doors, Heather cannot tell if she is laughing or screaming. Heather ducks and inches up to the picnic table as a shadow behind Sue, by the sink, beckons her. Thinking it must be Jason, Heather smiles, then shifts positions to see into the kitchen more clearly.

It is not Jason at the sink, but Joe. At first she thinks he is embracing Sue, and Heather's scalp contracts, but then Heather sees Sue's head waggle as Joe, teeth gritted, pectorals jumping, shakes her by the shoulders. Heather now understands that it is not rain on the window striping Sue's face, but tears.

Heather is surprised to find herself still poised on the lawn, the moon silvering her hands and arms as in a Diane Arbus photograph. The tableau in the kitchen has all the surreality and jerkiness of a foreign film, and Heather is willing to let the reel end. Besides, she fears that if she steps through the patio doors, everything between her and Joe will be different, irreconcilable. This is more than she bargained for when she agreed with the man in the diner, and now she longs to be pulling into the driveway again, then coming in through the front door as usual. But the consequences of that are also unbearably complex. The simplicity of the cold rain on her head seems perfect.

Heather thinks all of this very quickly; Joe still has his hands on Sue's shoulders. His face looks murky, undeveloped behind the wet window. The shadows on Joe's cheeks look like mutton-chop sideburns, on Sue's like too much blush. Blood rushes to the tip of Heather's nose as she tucks her chin to her chest and slides open the patio door.

"Joe," she says, and as her pupils contract in the bright light, she watches his face grow full and vividly familiar. In it, she recognizes Jason's eyes, Justin's chin and jaw. Relieved to discover that nothing fundamental has changed, she walks toward Joe and Sue with what she will come to call forgiveness.

COMMERCIALS

ON A THURSDAY EVENING in early November, the O'Conner family is clustered around the television set. They are watching Peter Sellers bumble his way through "A Shot in the Dark." One mishap leads to another until he is driving Elke Sommer away from a nudist colony in a little black Renault. Elke Sommer demurely covers her bare shoulders with her hands when people on the street crane their necks to look in the car windows. Mrs. O'Conner and her daughters giggle or chuckle; Mr. O'Conner crows. When it seems nothing else could go wrong for Peter Sellers, a squawking blackbird unexpectedly craps on his bowler hat. All of the O'Conners stamp their feet or shake with laughter. "You know what it is about Peter Sellers?" Mr. O'Conner asks. "He never gives up."

A commercial comes on: a woman stands with her hands on her hips smiling flirtatiously at a copier while a voice sings, "Try me. C'mon honey, try me." Miriam springs up to check the popcorn in the kitchen. Denise follows, her small hands fisted on her hips. They return to arrange paper napkins, bottles of Coke, and hot popcorn in front of the shuttered fireplace. Another commercial comes on. Two retired football players joke earnestly about their athletic reputations while they clutch bottles of light beer. Cathy raises her bottle of soda and takes a long drink, then roughly wipes her mouth with the back of her hand.

Mrs. O'Conner quickly surveys the faces of her family. Everyone is crunching popcorn and smiling. She remembers someone describing the television as an electronic hearth, and this image vaguely disturbs her. Its light is so cold. When the movie starts again, her family laughs loud and long.

Later, Margaret and Frank climb the stairs to their bedroom. Who can sleep? Frank wonders. He has been restless since his company reorganized and passed him over on the promotion ladder. Some days he feels strangely euphoric. Other days, he tells Margaret he feels all pent up. As Margaret undresses, Frank turns on a color portable to catch the late news. Instead, Channel 6 is showing an old movie. Frank sits on the edge of the bed and unlaces his shoes, watching Susan Hayward in "Back Street." She runs out of a beach house to greet a handsome man on a flagstone patio. He kisses his forefinger and presses it to her lips. A sea breeze rustles Susan Hayward's print dress, her eyes tear, then they embrace. Frank unbuckles his belt and props his head on the palms of his hands. Yawning, Margaret switches off the lamp and curls up under the sheets.

When the movies ends, Frank clicks off the set and rubs his eyes. Residual bits of light shimmer behind his eyelids. Who *wants* to sleep anymore, he thinks. Everything is changing. Hands out front like cartoon sleepwalker, Frank pads to the bathroom eerily illuminated by a streetlight. He separates a row of shampoo bottles on the windowsill to gaze at his neighbor's house. A downstairs window casts off the blue glow of a television set. Frank kisses his forefinger, then presses it to the glass, leaving a fish-shaped print in the condensation.

On Saturday morning, Miriam wakes and listens to the hum of the TV in the den beneath her bedroom. The branch of a larch tree scrapes against her window, but between the squeals of needles against the glass she hears cartoon theme music. She pulls the pillow over her ears. The canned laughter below sounds like the tinkle of glass breaking.

Miriam pushes open the swing door to the kitchen, and ducks under the swaying phone cord her mother has pulled across the room. Mrs. O'Conner sits at the kitchen table surrounded by newspaper sections, plates of cold toast, and half-filled glasses of orange juice. The zipper of his worn velour pullover is broken, and he slides the tab on one row of nylon teeth. Without looking up, he comments, "Got home a little late last night, did you?" Everything he says to Miriam lately sounds to him like clichéd father speeches. Knowing this aggravates his dismay and the distance between him and Miriam. I am getting too old, he thinks, to worry about being self-conscious.

Miriam opens a cupboard to reach for a coffee cup and replies, sharply and quietly, "Wasn't me. Must have been Mrs. Hanson from next door." Her words are muffled in the shelves.

Mr. O'Conner stares at his daughter, his eyes blank as buttons, and lifts a single eyebrow. This habit has creased only the right side of his forehead. "What's that?" he says loudly, glancing at his wife. He wads a paper napkin and rolls it into the butter dish.

Forget it, Dad," Miriam says, and turns away from him, facing the windows. Outside, the sky is matted gray with clouds. A chain on the clothesline pole rattles and clinks. Has my father always been this foolish? Miriam thinks, wincing. She sips her coffee and searches for the crossword puzzle in the sports section of the paper. Her father apologetically hands her a pencil. She lets it fall into her empty hand.

The day before, Miriam had walked into a coffee shop with her boyfriend, David, at a time when her father should have been at work. Instead, he sat in a red booth, holding hands with Mary Hanson. There was a basket of crackers and rolls on the table between them, and a mobile of brown and orange turkeys floating above their heads. Miriam grabbed David's arm and pulled him out of the restaurant before her father could see them.

Mrs. O'Conner hangs up the phone with a loud click and frowns at her husband. Lately, he is as impressionable as an adolescent, she thinks. The other day he came home with a baby blue cashmere cardigan. Claimed he saw Ralph Lauren wearing one on a commercial, and left promptly to buy one in the same color. He explained that he and Ralph Lauren have the same square face. Fiddling with the butter knife, Frank traces figure-eights through toast crumbs. He looks up helplessly at Miriam and Margaret.

"I'm going grocery shopping," Mrs. O'Conner announces. "We're out of everything."

As she leaves, Cathy walks into the kitchen on tiptoes, balancing her empty cereal bowl on her head. "I'm Cathy Rigby," she says, then leans against her father, peeking in his breast pocket. He used to bring her magic markers and slim calculators he filched from work. "Can we go next door again today and play with Nickelodeon?" Nickelodeon is the Hanson's English terrier, whose name is Michelob.

Miriam takes a drag on the cigarette her mother has left behind, crosses one arm over chest, and blows smoke into the air. She narrows her eyes and stares at her father. Stars of snow hit the glass of the window, stick there, then melt.

Miriam smashes the glowing tip of the cigarette into a puddle of coffee on her saucer and takes the newspaper into the den. On television, a man in a tux escorts a woman in silk pants through a hotel lobby, then turns when another woman's skirt swirls in the breeze created by the revolving doors, revealing her high-heeled, well-proportioned legs. Miriam flings the newspaper at the screen, then lowers the volume to call David.

Miriam is late for dinner. Her mother measures a sheet of plastic to wrap a casserole dish of mashed potatoes. Her husband sucks on a toothpick, slides the towel drawer in and out, and jiggles a screwdriver in his hand. He has had a bad day at work — one of the junior salesmen was promoted to sales manager. "What's wrong with this silly thing?" he grumbles, and squats down.

Mrs. O'Conner swings open the dishwasher, then puts her hand on her hip to greet Miriam. "Well, it's about time. Where have you been?"

Miriam unbuttons her coat slowly, shakes out her dark hair, and explains, "I was with David. We were looking at apartments." Her faces seems unnaturally pink. She smiles sympathetically at her mother, whose face is pinched with disappointment.

Mr. O'Conner, catching his finger in the drawer, howls. The screwdriver skitters across the counter, knocks into a box of toothpicks, and scatters them across the floor.

Mrs. O'Conner, hand still planted firmly on her hip, closes her eyes. Things were always easy before this winter, she thinks. Right?

"We found a nice place," Miriam continues. "We can move in as soon as the lease is signed." She smiles at her father, who looks up at her from the floor. He chomps on his toothpick furiously and watches his wife's face sag. "Do we have any boxes?" Miriam asks.

It is snowing. In front of the O'Conners' house, snow dusts the evergreens, rumples the lawn. Frank O'Conner is stooped on the driveway, tossing pebbles of salt on the asphalt.

A yellow school bus lets Cathy and Denise off at the corner and they trudge down the street in red galoshes. When they greet their father, he throws salt and says, "Why don't you go on in and help your mother?"

They find their mother in the kitchen, listening to lush music on the radio and chopping onions on a wooden board set over the sink. "Take off your boots in the hall, huh?" she says. Mrs. O'Conner brushes hair away from her face with the back of her hand and sniffles from the onions.

Denise finds a box of pretzels and sits cross-legged in front of a Dick Van Dyke rerun. When she and Cathy squabble, Denise realizes their mother is too quiet. She turns to Cathy with wide eyes, holds her finger to her lips, and offers Cathy some pretzels.

Mrs. O'Conner sets the table and tells Cathy to call her father in from outside.

"In a minute. Here comes the best part." Dick Van Dyke is discovering what is making the strange, other-worldly sound that has been haunting him.

Mrs. O'Conner, straw placemats in hand, marches into the den and snaps off the television. She turns abruptly to shoo her children into the kitchen as static recedes into the set.

"Aw, Mom," Denise wails, kicking a pillow against a chair.

"Mrs. O'Conner glares at her daughters and slaps the placemats down on an end table. Stop, stop, she thinks. She holds her left elbow with her right hand. "I'm going upstairs to lie down," she says, suddenly tired. "There's chicken on the table."

Denise and Cathy watch their mother slowly climb the stairs. Denise thinks the music on the radio makes her feel she and her mother and sister are in a made-for-TV movie. She sets four places on the round formica table and says to Cathy, "Go call Dad now."

Frank O'Conner calls his new lover from his office. After complaining about snow tires and snow plows, everyone else has gone to lunch.

"Mary?"

"Oh, hi, Frank."

When he hears her voice fall, his face droops. He has been rehearsing clever opening lines all morning. "Something wrong?" he asks.

"No, no, you just caught me at a bad time. Phil Donahue is interviewing child beaters."

"Sounds depressing. Say, listen. Why don't you cheer up and have lunch with me? I've got an extra chicken sandwich. What do you say? We could meet somewhere and eat in the car." Frank hears garbled applause in the phone.

"What?" Mary asks. "I'm sorry. A news flash. Olympic previews. Did you know I used to do gymnastics in high school? I was great on the parallel bars.

"I'll bet," Frank says, checking his watch. Through the phone lines, he hears a chorus singing, "Oh-o-o-oh what a feeling, to drive a Toyota." He imagines men leaping into the air in slow motion, fists clenched above their heads. "How 'bout it? Can you spare an hour for a rendezvous?" Frank knows Mary is enjoying the clandestine part of their relationship.

Mary whispers, "Yes. I think so. Herb won't be home until six. But I want to catch Dick Cavett later."

When they say goodbye, Frank waits to hear the click and buzz of her phone before he hangs up. He remembers the first time he kissed Mary two weeks ago. He loped across his back yard, the lawn crunchy with frost, to help her carry bags of groceries from her station wagon. The crispness of the air and the sudden heat in his muscles made him feel athletic and nostalgic for the games and fields of his youth. Surprising them both, Frank invited himself in for a cup of coffee. Mary unloaded cans of fruit cocktail and bags of elbow macaroni, and these small elements of her life seemed poignant and sweet to him. Frank, cheeks pink, measured vermouth and brandy for Manhattans. He tried to remember the name of the actor who played opposite Susan Hayward in that movie.

Alone with Mary in her kitchen, Frank found himself watching her more carefully than he ever had at any of their parties. She was trim, pert as a cheerleader. Something about the smoothness of her skin always made her look lightly tanned. Hadn't he dated someone named Mary in high school? He mentioned this to Mary, and she laughed, her mouth forming a coquettish O. Frank was aware that all the details of the moment — their spouses' absence, the chill of the day, the familiar weight of the grocery bags and the cadence of their flirtation — seemed staged and directed as if by a third person or a script. When Mary pried open a box of crackers and poured some onto a wooden platter, Frank circled his fingers around her wrist, rose from the chair, and kissed her noisily.

His hug upset the platter in her hand, and the little crackers plunked on the floor. He was relieved to hear Mary laugh quickly and girlishly, then joined in, their laughter billowing out of proportion to his clumsiness. Two hours and a few Manhattans later, Frank persuaded Mary to see how romantic an affair could be. He was surprised by his sincerity and persistence; when she warily led him up the stairs, he insisted she leave the bedroom window open to let the cold breeze flutter her print curtains. She kissed his fingers hesitantly, then let him pull her down onto the sunny bed. He thought he had never enjoyed lovemaking as much as that afternoon. Her reluctance made him feel extraordinary and virile when she finally gave in.

Now, in his office, reliving that afternoon, Frank tries to mimic the leap frozen in his imagination. He crouches, then springs into the air. His jump doesn't have the ease of suspension he imagined, and he knocks over a wastebasket on his way down, but he grins broadly anyway. He punches his right fist into his left palm. "You are one lucky man," he chuckles, "and you don't give up."

Margaret O'Conner waits until Denise and Cathy have finished their lunch before she uses the phone in the kitchen. She slips their milky glasses and plates under a veil of white suds, then dials her daughter's new number.

"Miriam?"

"Mom. How are you?"

Margaret is relieved to hear that her daughter's voice is still uncharacteristically deep. Everything else is changing beyond her control. "Oh, fine. And you? How are things with your roommate?"

"David? Everything's just fine with David. We're still unpacking, you know, but we're getting there. How's Dad?"

Margaret parts the curtains to see Frank stalk a pile of snowy bricks. "You know your father. He's tinkering around with something out back, as usual."

Miriam gasps, then tries to mask it with a cough.

"Listen, would you like to come for Thanksgiving dinner next week? David too?" Margaret hears a familiar commercial for a pain reliever on the television in the empty den and through the phone lines in Miriam's new apartment. She imagines all the people in her family, in her neighborhood, in the country, linked by common televised images. She wonders if this creates more or less fellow-feeling among viewers. Less, she supposes.

"Sure," Miriam agrees. "Thanksgiving sounds great." Both endure a long pause. "Hey, Mom," Miriam continues. "How well do you know the Hansons next door?"

Involuntarily, Margaret's eyes lift and she peers out the patio doors in the kitchen to watch Mary Hanson drive off in her station wagon. Margaret checks the time on the wall clock. "They're just neighbors, Miriam. Herb and I don't really get along." She rolls the ashes off her cigarette. "Why do you ask?" Margaret hears her daughter clear her throat.

"Well," Miriam begins. "I was wondering if I could borrow their wheelbarrow."

Margaret turns and walks to the sink, where she runs her cold water over her wrists. The cigarette bobs on her lips as she says, "You'll have to ask your father. He knows the Hansons better than I do."

When they hang up, Margaret paces, then settles back in her chair, one arm crossed over her chest, one crooked, holding a cigarette in midair. Blowing smoke through her nostrils, she stamps the cigarette out on the floor. Closing her eyes and grimacing, she arches her back, then rushes into the den to snap off the television set.

Miriam hangs up the phone and watches David's curly head silhouetted against a black and white television screen. On a table in front of him, he has laid out newspapers so that he can glue the sides of a desk drawer onto their mahogany front. "That was your mother on the phone?"

Miriam sits at the large dining room table across from him. She too has laid out newspapers to pot and repot plants. She takes a manicure scissors and snips dry leaves from a Chinese evergreen. "Uh huh. Wants us to come for Thanksgiving." She scoops up a handful of dirt and clenches it in her fist. "I should have told her about Dad and Mary Hanson."

David takes a thin paint brush and daubs epoxy onto wood. "Maybe she already knows. All she has to do is look out the kitchen window at the right time."

Miriam crumbles the moist soil and lets it sift through her fingers and into the pot. "Listen, David," she begins with determination. "There are still some things we haven't worked out here." She holds out her soiled hand in an awkward pose. It looks gray in the flickering TV light. She rubs some dirt into a ball, trying to phrase a definitive statement.

David rises, smiling, and, standing behind her, loops both arms around Miriam. He kisses her where she has parted her dark hair. "Miriam, Miriam, don't be such a worry wart."

She turns to face him, and absentmindedly wipes her hand on his shirt. David laughs and shakes his head. As they kiss, the AT&T jingle — Reach Out — starts up, and Miriam rolls her eyes at the parallel between the sentimental lyrics and her actions. She turns off the television and persuades David to go out for lunch. At the restaurant, they run into Ron and Patty, mutual friends, and Miriam grows sullen when David turns down an opportunity to play racquetball so that he can return home to watch a college basketball game.

Denise comes home late on a Friday night. She and her friend Juli have been secretly smoking cigarettes and drinking beer in Juli's garage. Before Denise enters the den, she sniffs her hair for the scent of smoke. She worries that she smells too much like mint, so she drinks a glass of water in the darkened kitchen.

Denise is relieved to find only her father in the family room sitting with two stacks of Consumer Reports magazines on either side of his chair. He is leafing through all the issues of the year; he is thinking of buying.

Moving very slowly, Denise leans back into the cushions of the sofa.

"So, Denise, what did you and Juli do tonight?"

"Oh, nothing. Played games with her little brother. She got a new deluxe Monopoly for her birthday last week."

None of this is true. They avoided Juli's brother; the birthday party was a fabricated excuse to have a similar evening last weekend. Juli owns a deluxe Monopoly set, but it is years old.

"Your mother and I are going to Beloit tomorrow to see your aunt and uncle. Do you want to come?" He picks at some of the loose threads of his terrycloth bathrobe.

Denise looks hard into the television set. "No, I have homework to do." This too is a lie. Already Denise is thinking of calling Juli. The problem is getting Cathy out of the way.

A girl in a blue bathing suit plays water volleyball with boys her age. Two boxes of tampons are superimposed on the splashing pool water. Denise slumps down, and jerks her hand up to her cheek to cover her face. Next, two women in almost transparent pastel dresses walk through a park. In muted tones, they talk about feminine protection. Denise rocks her left leg across her right knee.

Mr. O'Conner looks up from his magazine. "I've never understood why a woman would want to buy that stuff," he says, trying to find sympathy in his daughter.

Instead, she stands up and tramps out of the room. As she leaves, she calls, "Oh, Dad, don't you know anything?"

The next morning, Denise and Cathy are awakened by the rumble of their parents' argument in the kitchen beneath their bedroom. Cathy props herself up on one elbow when she hears drawers slam and chairs screech across the linoleum. She can't hear what they are saying, but her eyes sting with tears when she hears a thud and the chime of glass breaking.

"Denise? You awake? Mom's mad."

"Go back to sleep. It's early yet."

The shrill, discordant tones of the O'Conners' argument rise through the floorboards.

"But Denise, I can't sleep with all this ruckus."

The word "ruckus" makes them both break into giggles.

"C'mon then," Denise whispers. "We'll watch TV until this blows over."

Carrying their pillows into their parents' bedroom, they stop in the hall to listen to the argument.

". . . around here, and I can't even get ahold of you on the phone."

Something metallic spins with a ring, then clatters to the floor. Cathy runs into the bedroom, turns on the set, leaving the volume on low, and covers her ears with the corners of the pillow. Denise follows and quietly closes the door behind her.

Denise realizes this means she will have to go to Beloit. She lies back and pounds her heels against the floor. Things were so much better when Dad wasn't around so much of the time, she thinks. Why doesn't he get another job, or find a hobby that he has to do away from the house?

Denise feels the queasiness of guilt when she hears the stomping of footsteps on the stairs. Cathy curls up behind the pillow when her father swings the door open.

"Get downstairs and help your mother clean up." His voice fills the whole room. "And get dressed quick. We're all going to Beloit."

In Beloit, Margaret's sister and her family cheer them all. Her husband collects and sells antique music boxes and old musical instruments. He explains this business to Frank and Margaret over coffee while Denise and Cathy play with the slot machines and pinball games in the basement. When they tire of this, they turn on a twelve-inch TV sitting on top of an old stove. They watch a trailer for Charlie Chan theater. Charlie Chan stalks a crippled killer through the maze of a hospital's boiler room. Denise and Cathy stalk each other through the strange pantries and rec room. Denise finds a Mason jar of preserved pears and, not even hungry, she knocks the lid against the linoleum floor to open it, then eats some pears with her fingers. Cathy, at first refusing, finally plunges her hand into the sticky jar and pulls out three pear halves. She licks her fingers dramatically and giggles.

Later, on the way home in the car, the O'Conners stop at a rest station to refuel. Cathy bounces on her seat, then yanks the door open. "I have to use the bathroom," she calls out.

In the gas station, she finds herself alone in the room where bags of Fritos and barbecued potato chips are sold. Cathy grabs two sticks of Beef Jerky and a bag of Doritos, slips them into her coat pocket, then skips back to the car.

When her parents argue in the front seat over which exit to take, Cathy unzips her pocket to show Denise her booty. Denise's eyes widen, then she cups her hand over her mouth to stifle a laugh. They open the packages under their skirts to muffle the crinkle of the cellophane.

*   *   *

58

Preparing for bed, Margaret stands by the nighttable and smooths hand cream over her wrists and knuckles, her brow involuntarily furrowed with worry. As Frank hops out of his pants, change jingles in his pockets, then spills out on the bedspread. He remembers crackers skittering, and dives for the bouncing coins, grinning. Outside, the wind sculpts snow into dunes.

Frank turns off the lights, twists the knob of the TV set and stares. In a commercial for a upcoming movie, a girl in a string bikini, her mouth smeared with lipstick in an imitation of sultriness, flounces up to an older man. She pushes his glasses askew and cocks her head seductively to kiss him for a long time. "Jeez, look at this," Frank says. "Haven't commercials gotten more suggestive lately? Like in the last month or so?" Margaret shrugs. "Must have missed the new FCC ruling," Frank claims and climbs into bed, then folds back the covers and pats the mattress, smiling up at his wife. She adjusts the volume, crawls across the bed, and slips under the covers.

"There we go," Frank says, yawning. "It's been a long, hard day. We both need a good night's sleep."

Margaret doesn't reply. She is watching Elke Sommer talk to Johnny Carson. She looks at Elke's face very carefully to see if she has changed since Peter Sellers. It could be the makeup, and it could be the lights, but Elke looks the same — younger if that's possible.

Margaret turns her head to look at her husband. His eyes are already closed, his mouth slack with sleep. "Frank?" she nudges him.

"What, what?" Frank says, kicking the covers.

Margaret picks at pills of wool on the blanket.

"What is it, honey? I was just falling asleep."

Margaret moves to her husband and presses her fingers on his asymmetrically-lined forehead. She is waiting for the courage to say the words she has been rehearsing all day. "Don't go to sleep yet. Look, Elke Sommer is on the Tonight Show."

"Elke Sommer?" He sits up, peers at the screen with bleared eyes. Elke Sommer is swinging a smooth leg through a slit in her silk skirt. She is laughing so hard that she can't finish her sentence. Johnny Carson turns a deadpan face to the camera. Frank slumps down and rolls over. Margaret reaches under the covers and strokes his bent leg. She licks circles in his ear.

After a shot of Doc Severinson in a velvet tunic, Frank begins to snore. Margaret elbows him the ribs. "I told you not to go to sleep yet," Margaret whispers, teeth clenched.

"Margaret," Frank sighs. He takes her hand and kisses it, then cups it between his own, as if he were praying.

Margaret watches lights turn on and off next door, then, watching Frank's familiar features relax unfamiliarly, she disentangles her hand from his and goes into the bathroom. Turning on the water, she drops down on the bathtub ledge, begins to cry, and brings the heel of her hand up to her eyes.

On Thanksgiving Day, David drives Miriam to her parents' house. The sky is clear, and the bright snow on the ground makes her squint. It is Miriam's first visit; she brings the Chinese evergreen as a gift for her mother, and a large, boxed jigsaw puzzle for her sisters.

When they open the door, a smell of simmering onions and turkey rubbed with sage greets them. Miriam's sisters and parents crowd the hall. Everyone kisses her; her mother accepts the plant, then combs her fingers through Miriam's hair and admires its new cut. Mr. O'Conner shakes David's hand.

Cathy serves hor'd'oerves to people huddled around a card table where Miriam has set up the jigsaw puzzle of fruit spilling out of a straw cornucopia. Giant Mickey Mouse and Donald Duck balloons bob down Fifth Avenue in New York City. Miriam immediately finds a piece that snaps into place, and she smiles. It feels good to be home, she thinks. Then Mr. O'Conner wriggles a whole group of pieces, the purple grapes, into place. Everyone cheers. In the kitchen, Mrs. O'Conner munches on a stalk of celery and sips from a tumbler of scotch and water

David joins Mrs. O'Conner in the kitchen. The noise from the other room is beginning to bother her and she pours more scotch.

"Sure smells good in here," David remarks. He picks up an olive and pops it into his mouth.

"Oh, it should. The turkey's been cooking for hours." She tips a bottle of wine toward him. "Care for a drink?"

She watches as he pours and she thinks, Miriam chose this man. This man, David, and Miriam. She wishes she were poised again on the brink of the decision to marry Frank — she would have been firmer about certain things. She blinks when David straightens up, then begins to whip the potatoes.

Miriam and her sisters are still chattering over the puzzle when their father turns to watch a commercial. A young Olympic gymnast spins and bounces on a pair of parallel bars. Older and a mother now, she confides to the viewer that she still eats the cereal from her childhood.

Mr. O'Conner tugs on his earlobe and slips quietly upstairs. Even though she is busy talking to David and cooking, Margaret sees Frank pass the open kitchen door.

She drops the mushrooms she is washing into cold water, walks past David leaning on the counter, and picks up the phone to hear her husband say, "Mary?" on the upstairs extension. She pushes down the clear button first, then replaces the receiver. David watches her rip a shred of loose skin from her thumb with her teeth, then yank back the curtains to look out across the back yard.

Her face clouding, Margaret runs into the family room, kicks over the card table and screams, "Frank! Goddamn you, Frank O'Conner."

Her children pick up velveteen pillow cushions to hide their faces. David moves his chair in the kitchen so that he can see Margaret's livid face in the den. Keeping his eyes on her, he sips his warm wine. Miriam peeks out from under a cushion and picks a puzzle piece out of Cathy's curls. Her mother kicks off the TV.

"Frank," Margaret yells. She runs to the closet, pulls on her coat, then hollers up from the foot of the stairs, "This is it, Frank."

In the kitchen, den, and bedroom, everyone sits as if paralyzed, listening to Margaret O'Conner start her car and back it down the driveway.

Frank O'Conner descends the stairs sheepishly and finds his daughters huddled around the opened oven, arguing quietly about what to do with the turkey.

Hours later, it has begun to snow. The walk in front of the O'Conners' door has patches of rough ice. The larch tree bends and sways against a darkening sky. Snow falls like mist in front of the headlights of Margaret O'Conners car.

She finds her family watching the news. Someone has cleaned

the den and the kitchen too. Margaret pulls off her gloves and listens to the weatherman predict snow, snow, and more snow.

"Hi, Mom," Cathy ventures, looking stunned and guilty.

"Miriam and David left. They waited a long time, though," Denise offers.

"Did you girls eat?" Margaret asks quietly. They shake their heads. "Well, c'mon then. We'll cut up some turkey."

Frank stands and slides a pen in and out of his shirt pocket. He watches his wife pull her daughters off of the couch.

Margaret sets the table for three and puts out bowls of mashed potatoes, cranberry sauce, and sweet corn. She slices the cool turkey and gives each daughter three pieces.

Frank paces in the den, finds himself snapping his fingers in time to a catchy theme song.

As her children eat, Margaret tells them she went to the neighborhood SuperAmerica, waiting there for their father to come and find her. Because he didn't, he was going to move away for awhile. Cathy and Denise chew their food slowly.

Frank pokes his head into the kitchen. "What's that?" His face is flushed, his eyes too bright.

Margaret slices her piece of turkey into tiny pieces, looks at her husband, and says, "You heard me, Frank. It won't work. Twenty years and this just won't work." Her throat is salty with tears.

Frank stares at the table. Everything looks very white, over-focused. He feels himself waiting for the camera to stop rolling, or the channels to change. Blinking, he returns to the den, picks up bits of paper and balls of thread on the carpet. He had already persuaded himself it is someone else's marriage that is breaking up. He mulls over what Mary had said on the phone, before Margaret broke in. "Our affair has been played out." How do women know these things?

Fiddling with the erratic color on the set, Frank forms apologetic, humble speeches in his mind. "Margaret," he thinks, then, "Mary." He listens to his wife click her cutlery against her plate. Then, watching his jaunty figure in the reflection of the TV screen, he parts the curtains in the den and winks out the window. Remembering Peter Sellers' persistence and feeling superstitious and lucky, Frank crouches down on the rug, and pushes himself off his feet, fist clenched above his head. When he punches the ceiling, bits of plaster snow down on his head.

LEAVE OF ABSENCE

"I'M SICK OF COLLEGE TOWNS," I tell Richard on the telephone. "The fraternity boys leave dead animals on their rivals' lawns, sneak into parties and pour more grain alcohol than anyone can handle into the punch." What I neglect to tell Richard is that I'm frightened by the fraternity boys, my neighbors, and when I'm frightened, I flee.

Through the static, I hear Richard laugh. "They're lining the entire valley with boutiques filled with New Wave furniture and grim-looking mannequins. How many expensive kitchen supply stores and yuppie stationers can the world take?"

"Carrie," Richard says, then sighs as if he were blowing into a shell.

"I'm starting my leave of absence from work next week, but I've got nowhere to go. I want to get away from here and write a story or two."

"Come to Maine," Richard suggests. "Bring your typewriter and we'll fix you up just fine."

"Okay," I say. I imagine Richard surrounded by water, and my memories of our past misunderstandings quiver and burst like balloons. "Can you help me scrounge up some odd jobs?"

I smuggle my cat onto the Greyhound bus in a Bean's tote bag and sit next to a startled-looking man drinking lemonade from a waxed carton. His neck and hands are stained with dark brown splotches shaped like tobacco leaves. He blinks at my cat and asks, "Visiting friends in Portland?"

I shake my head and think too long about the first part of his question. Richard is both more and less than a friend; we console one another when we are unhappy, but our familiarity and the distances between us can make us wary and secretive. "Not Portland," I finally reply. "Chebeague Island." I inadvertantly mispronounce it.

The man smacks his lips and pushes his seat back. "Sha-beague," he corrects me. He lights a cigarette and pinches it delicately between his thumb and forefinger.

I buy a one-way ferry ticket from a sunburned woman sitting on a stool shucking peanuts, then lean against a weathered post and squint to see if Richard is working the incoming boat. I can make out a woman having difficulty folding a newspaper in the wind, and a tall man in a fishing hat carrying a blonde girl on his shoulders. Then my head goes light when I see Richard uncoiling a heavy rope. I watch the wrinkles of his slicker fill in with light and shadow as the boat floats near, and consider I might be happy if time and space were immediately suspended, preserving the perfect dull shine of the bay and my own buoyancy as Richard floats ever toward me, full of the possible.

The ferry shudders up the narrow channel and bumps against the dock, then Richard and a skinny man with a Stan Laurel grin tie the boat to the posts. "Welcome aboard," Richard says, and salutes me with a smile. His face is the same: open and weathered. When I recognize his clean smell of castile soap and sand, years drain away. There is an awkward moment before we decide to kiss hastily, then let the slight list of the boat part us.

I find a bench at the stern and rearrange the cat in my lap, then close my eyes and listen for the hoot of the boat's whistle. The wind lifts my hair, rushes around my ears. When I open my eyes, I notice the blue sky is streaked white with clouds like whittled ribs.

Richard crouches in front of me and steadies himself by holding onto the underside of the bench.

"Took a mess of clams out of cold storage this morning," he says. His dark hair feathers in the wind. "And we just brought in a new shipment of Soave." A blue vein pulses in the tanned skin of his temple.

"You're too good to me," I say, but a blast of the boat's horn drowns out my words.

Richard looks up toward the prow. "Been asking around about jobs for you."

I pull a hank of hair out of my eyes and chew my lip. "Yeah?"

Richard holds his thumb out to count. "Owen Fickett's wife, Barbara, has multiple sclerosis and needs someone to care for her while Owen is away this summer. Talk to him first and see what he expects."

Richard holds up his index finger. "The Inn's serving pizza now. They might need a part-time cheese grater. And you can always dig clams. Fifty dollars for two buckets."

"Sounds good. Thanks."

Richard stands up, straightens his khaki pants, and says, "Everything'll be just fine. No one goes hungry on the island." The he leaves to heave the lines down below. I look up at the screeching seagulls wheeling above me, see the ruggedly scalloped rocks of Chebeague, and wonder, love?

Richard pulls open the door of his '67 Galaxie and places my bags on the back seat. He lets out the choke slowly, listens to it gasp, then rams the shift down on the steering column. He drives carefully along the crumbling asphalt roads and waves to people bouncing by in pickup trucks.

Richard shifts into second, pushes his blue trucker's hat down so that the visor covers his eyebrows. "Want to see the rest of the island," he asks, then adds, "we're heading toward the outback."

"Take me anywhere," I say. The cat hugs the floormat and stares at me with plaintive eyes.

As Richard identifies the single church, the dump, the eccentric cartoonist's house, I sit back and let my arm trail out the window. The land becomes hard, scrabbly. Milkweed and prickly lettuce choke the gulleys at the side of the road. Gravel crunches and pops against the fenders. The sea wind has triggered my dormant sensors, and I take the island in greedily and immediately, through my pores.

"This is the West End, Chandler's Cove," Richard explains. We are perched on a rocky rise, looking down on purplish water dotted with anchored lobster boats. The air smells washed, salty; it makes my skin bloom. My bones are loose, unhinged; my legs feel like unfurled rope. If Richard kissed me now, we both might rise up out of the car and skim across the bay, defying gravity.

Instead, he eases the car into reverse. "Home, madam?" he asks, then shifts and heads back east. Watching the shrubs shiver in the early evening wind, I realize I have not eaten all day and I'm famished.

I poke around Richard's kitchen while he washes romaine and slices tomatoes for a salad. When I switch on the radio to hear Frankie Ford sing the original Sea Cruise, Richard boils sea water for the clams.

After dinner we place our empty plates on the floor for the cat to lick, then wrap ourselves in afghans on the living room sofa as the chill night air seeps in.

"So, you're not in love," Richard says, balancing his wineglass on his covered knee.

"No, I'm thinking of giving up on all that," I reply playfully. "Massachusetts was not good to me."

Richard laughs, then pauses and says, "Maine has been good to me, but I'm thinking of giving it up anyway. Living on an island is tough. You've got to take everything into your own hands."

I wriggle my fingers in the open weave of the afghan on Richard's knee. He sips his wine, then sucks the wet curls of his moustache. "I've been living alone a long time, Carrie," he explains.

I withdraw my hand and stare at shadows in my lap. "How 'bout you, I ask. Have you fallen in or out of love lately?"

Richard bends forward to drain the contents of the wine bottle into his glass, then twists to look at me. "Kindness is the one essential thing," he states, enunciating each word carefully, "that people overlook when they are falling out of love."

My question drifts like nets in water. Richard eases himself back into the pillows, and, with his face flushed, wipes off the condensation on the wineglass with his thumb.

The cat crawls from under the sofa, greets us with a muted trill, then settles herself on a plaited placemat on the dining room table. I am puzzled. Was I unkind to Richard years ago when I was the first to leave? I was frightened then — Richard had spoken of marriage — and I flew to Rome impulsively with all of my savings. I never really offered an explanation, just opulent postcards from Europe. Richard wrote me long revelatory letters which I didn't receive until I returned home and never acknowledged because they looked crumpled and anachronistic.

I stand, stretch, then slump back down. The country music on the radio makes me sleepy and hopeful. "Will you show me to my room," I ask, mock formal.

Richard drapes the afghan across his shoulders and leads me upstairs. "Here you be," he says, and turns on the light. He stands with his hand on the doorknob and I duck past him, thinking he might follow. But he closes the door, and I am alone in the cold room.

A double bed with a white chenille bedspread stands next to a curtained window. I pile one pillow on top of the other and discover a cheesy postcard of a gigantic lobster tucked under the sheet. Welcome to Chebeague, Richard has written.

As I switch off the light, there is a soft knock at the door. The white blanket on Richard's shoulders and the yellow lamp in the hall seem to fill the entire room with light. Already I can feel his warm hands on my shoulders, his lips against my neck. "Call the Ficketts tomorrow," he reminds me.

I nod and close the door. This is Maine; keep it slow, I think, then sink into soft dark dreams.

Alone in Richard's kitchen, I watch the morning fog lift, snap the ends off beans, then call Owen Fickett.

"Call back tomorrow," he says mysteriously.

I remember feeling suspended the day before on the Portland dock — now I yearn for resolution, hard and dry as stones. I rehearse a speech, gesticulating over the sink. I had to do some things, I'll say, traveling, writing. But now that I'm here, I'll go out on a limb. Love, I think, stumped, searching for the one right phrase that will make it easy.

Distracted, I head upstairs to my typewriter, and write until I fall asleep in my dirty clothes, long before Richard docks the last ferry.

The next morning I wake early and decide I've been foolish; Richard is hospitable and generous, but he is not in love with me. Thinking it best to leave Richard's before things grow too tense, I walk to Owen Fickett's house, and wave to a man in a terrycloth hat riding a lime-green John Deere lawnmower. He leans forward, grimaces up at the sky, and turns the machine off. He sits back, wipes his face with his hat, and waits for me to approach.

"Mr. Fickett," I say, extending my arm. "Carrie Cunningham."

We shake hands. His skin is pale and pasty, although the sun is bright.

"I was wondering when you'd come by," he says heartily, lisping slightly.

I smile, bemused, and slap a mosquito on my shin. A rash of sweat breaks out over his upper lip.

"Well, come inside and I'll show you what needs to be done."

As I follow him up the lawn, I notice his green shirt is stained with crescents of perspiration and that he is wearing canvas slippers.

On the porch he squeezes the handle of the screen door and whispers, "My wife has multiple sclerosis, and I'm leaving tomorrow for Connecticut to teach summer school." He fumbles in his shirt pocket for a cigarette and places it, unlit, between his lips. "She needs someone to stay with her at night, help her dial the phone, make meals, stuff like that. My two kids used to stay with her, but this year, the boy got a job and my daughter. . . well, let's just say she got her heart broken on the island and hasn't been back since." He kicks a stone into a cedar bush. "Que séra, séra, right?" He winks and holds the door open for me.

Inside, everything is covered in a fine plaster dust. *Yankee* magazines are piled on top of a blue radiator. Owen shows me around the house.

"And here we have the dining room," he booms, wringing his hands. "And this tiny space used to be the kitchen, until I built this." He pushes a swing door dramatically, grins, and follows me into a kitchen crowded with dark brown appliances. A cookie jar with a ceramic monkey holding its hands over its eyes sits in the middle of the large table. Wallpaper printed with red coffee grinders decorates the walls. A fragile black-haired woman wearing two blue sweaters and brown stretch pants balances between the stove and a lowered slate countertop.

"You must be Barbara Fickett," I say.

"Yes," she replies, and leans forward to grasp my hand. She slides into a heavy wooden chair and gazes at me with smudged eyes. "So you're here for the summer," she asks. "Writing?" she props her chin with the back of her fist.

I move a plastic vacuum cleaner attachment from a chair, sit, and say, "Yes."

Owen pushes a rack of dirty dishes into an opened dishwasher, eats a soggy Oreo cookie, and says, "Some kitchen, eh? I designed it myself so my wife could always hold onto something." As he chews, I notice a tuft of gray hair under his nose.

"By the way, been to Portland?" he asks. "They're really fixing the town up. Go to a store like the Whisk and the Spoon to stock a kitchen like this." He laughs, a rough wheezing laugh like the cartoon dog on the Jetsons.

Barbara smiles as me. "There's lots to do around here," she murmurs. "You know the poet ...."

"Yes, the fellow with the beard," Owen interrupts. "You know. Who wrote *Leaves of Grass?*"

"Whitman," I say.

"No, no, the other one," Owen says, snapping his fingers. "Well, he's got a house right around here anyway."

"Longfellow," Barbara offers.

Owen throws a spoon into the stainless steel sink. "I knew it, he says, pounding the countertop with the side of his hand. It was right on the tip of my tongue. Henry Woodsworth Longfellow." Owen pivots to face me. "Now what did he write?"

"Poetry," I say, standing.

Barbara slowly turns to watch a pair of finches flutter around a birdfeeder. Owen crumples a crumbed piece of waxed paper, then says, "Would you like to see your room?"

I follow him up a curving staircase, plumes of dust puffing from the thick gray carpeting. "And here we are," Owen says through clenched teeth. He is having trouble with the rusted hook on the door. Finally the door springs open to reveal a perfectly square room with a single high round window. The air smells like scorched rubber and wet sawdust.

"You can set up your typewriter right here," Owen declares, dusting a small metal desk. "And there's plenty of closet space." He jerks back a plastic shower curtain to show me the closet. "Now you don't have to spend all of your time here. I'll be around on the weekends and you can come and go as you please." He pokes my shoulder and adds in a lowered voice, "I will ask you to do one thing for me."

"What's that," I ask, looking down at his slippers.

"Pick the peas in the backyard. They're just about ready to go."

"Fine," I say. The unpicked peas make my decision to pull away form Richard irreversible.

"Why don't we go get your things?" Owen claps me on the back. "I've got a few minutes now."

"Fine," I say again. "I'd like to bring everything over at once."

"As you like." He winks at me. "We'll show that heartbreaker."

He drives me home, then waits in his smoke-gray Subaru while I pack. Folding shorts and T-shirts into a backpack, I think, it won't be so bad if he's not around. Better to leave now than let things build to a head with Richard. On the front porch, the cat is curled in a yellow square of sun. She jerks up and stares at Owen when he loads my pack into his trunk.

"Why don't you come by tonight after dinner? Then you can just stay over." He fiddles with a loose button on his shirt.

"I've got dinner guests tonight," I apologize. "It will probably go pretty late."

Owen shrugs. "I'm always up until eleven."

I nod. "I'll be by in the morning."

Owen climbs into the car and slams the door. "Suit yourself," he says, then backs down the driveway, gravel sputtering under his tires.

Richard arrives home early lugging a plastic white bucket filled with lobsters. "K.C. will be here soon," he informs me, and pulls a copper-bottomed kettle out of the cupboard, clanging it against the sink. I pare an eggplant, rinse potatoes for the ratatouille, and rehearse my farewell speech to Richard.

We hear K.C. cutting through the woods; twigs snap and dead branches creak. "Smells good in there," he yells, sniffing at the screen door. I clamp a lid on the stew and rush into the hall. I am surprised I have to strain to embrace K.C.; I have forgotten how big he is. "Well, look at you," he says, and whistles. He plucks a corner of my second-hand cotton dress. "Regular countrified." Richard emerges from the living room with an Emmy Lou Harris album tucked under his arm, and shakes K.C.'s hand. K.C. pulls at his gold seaman's earring in his left ear, and nods toward the record. "There we go," he says emphatically. "Best voice this side of California." In the cramped, dim hallway, we all laugh.

K.C. bows and kisses my hand. "It's good to see you two together again," K.C. says. Richard surprises me by squeezing my hand and rubbing my arm.

K.C. beams, runs a hand through his shaggy hair, and strides to the bathroom. "Your shower still working, Ricardo," he asks, then pokes his head into the kitchen. "Best shower this side of California," he explains. Richard and I laugh, smile at one another, and shake our heads. When I hear the spray of the shower spatter against the porcelain, I melt butter for the lobsters, light candles in the kitchen.

Richard plays the Emmy Lou Harris album and pulls me into the dining room where he waltzes me around the table, and croons softly, his lips grazing my cheek, until we hear the sizzle of butter burning in the kitchen. I hurry to turn off the flame and, in the reflection of a dark window, catch Richard staring at me wistfully.

"Richard," I say, flushed in the candlelight. "I'll go out on a limb."

His hands are warm on my shoulders, his lips soft, soft. "Love," he whispers. We hold each other until we hear the shower squeak off.

During dinner, K.C. tells us stories about his last six months on board ship. "The worst job," he explains, "was climbing down to the bilge and swabbing up leaking fuel oil and other crud. Wouldn't believe the fumes. Couldn't have been healthy." K.C. stares at the cracked lobster carcass on his plate. He turns to me abruptly and asks, "You found any work yet?"

Glancing apologetically at Richard, I describe my job at the Ficketts'. Richard listens carefully as he picks out white shreds of lobster and feeds them to my patient cat.

"Wait a minute," K.C. warns. "Every night over there? How much they paying you?"

I try to remember if I discussed a salary with Owen and realize that in my haste to elude him, I neglected that crucial detail. I check my watch, see that it is already after midnight, and say, "I'll call him in the morning."

K.C. and Richard look at me with mock sternness.

"Well, it's got to be at least fifty dollars a week," I say, dismissing them, understanding that Owen probably does not intend to pay me at all.

"Cunningham," K.C. says with a snort, "sometimes I don't know about you."

"Listen," Richard warns. "Maybe I was wrong to recommend the Ficketts. She's wonderful, very bright, and I thought you two would get on. But Owen." Richard looks at K.C. for confirmation. "Owen's been known to be a bit stingy, nasty too. He'd tie the world up in a bow and give it to his wife if he could, but he can be spiteful and mean if you trouble him." Richard sighs. "Just be diplomatic when you call him."

Richard rises to scrape the dishes and gather lobster rinds to be sunk at high tide. Then we walk K.C. to the door and turn the porch light on. "Call when you get real work," he chides me.

I follow Richard into the front room, where he sits on the sofa. "Listen, I don't have to go over there," I say.

After a few quiet moments, Richard pulls me close and says, "Does Owen know how well you know me?"

I shrug. "I didn't say anything," I explain.

"Good. It's better not to mention it."

I wait for an explanation, or a sign.

"See, I dated his daughter a bit last summer and he didn't like it at all. Not at all. Doesn't really like Chebeaguers. Specially me."

My fingers are knotted and nervous. I swallow and say, "He mentioned his daughter had a broken heart."

"Huh. That's what he said." Richard disentangles himself from me and paces the room. "That's a strange way of looking at it." He cranes his neck, touches the window glass tentatively. "She really threw me for a loop, that one. Up and left the island just as we were getting involved, a real romance. Never heard from her again."

My cheeks are still stinging from the sudden revelation of Richard's secret romance. "So it ended just like that," I say.

Richard stands by the dark window. "Not quite. I had a hard time of it. Mooned about, couldn't sleep for days." He presses his forehead against the glass. "One night I gathered up all the things she's given me — a sweater, some dried flowers, old books, a funny straw hat." I see his small smile reflected against the night sky.

"I put all of this stuff in a cardboard box," Richard continues, "and waited until dark. I remember that there was almost no wind that night. I cut through the yards to the Ficketts', dug a shallow hole under her window, and doused the box with gasoline. That's when Owen found me. He chased me down to the road and told me she'd left the night before."

"That's sad," I say.

"No. Not sad. Just hard." Richard sits next to me and shakes his head. "But all the women I've ever loved have left me," he says softly. "You too."

"Richard," I begin.

"Stay here," Richard says, holding my hand between his palms.

"Okay," I say. "Okay."

I rise out of Richard's bed early the next morning and call the Ficketts. "Mr. Fickett," I say. "Carrie Cunningham."

"Carrie? I kept the porch light on for you all night." He laughs a beat too late.

I wipe the dust off the telephone dial with the belt of my bathrobe and say, "Listen, I forgot to ask you yesterday in all the commotion what the, uh, compensation for the job will be." In the moment of silence that follows, my neck flushes with a vague fear.

"Well, room and board," Owen says, a bit too astonished. "You know, you have your own room and all you can eat. And you can come and go as you please. No hassles."

I say, "I couldn't possibly do it for that. You see, my room and board are already provided." I am surprised at how cool I sound.

"You're better off getting out of there," Owen insists. He clears his throat, rales, then asks roughly, "What do you think is reasonable? Compensation, I mean."

"I'd say about fifty dollars a week."

"Goodness," Owen exclaims. "Just for sleeping here at night? That's two hundred and fifty dollars. I couldn't afford that."

"Sorry," I say.

"Well, cripes," Owen says, drawing out the grating sound of the initial letters. He whispers, "She's sitting right here."

"I'm sorry," I say again, "but I really do need the money and you are asking. . . ."

"All right. Suit yourself," Owen says angrily. "You've been talking to Richard, huh? I told you to come by last night." His receiver must have bumped something because there is a loud crack in my ear. "I'll show you. You can come by and pick up your own damn stuff."

"Excuse me," I ask politely, but Owen has already hung up the phone.

When Richard calls from Portland later, I tell him the story of the Ficketts as if it were a joke with a punch line. "'Crrripes,' he said, just like that, Richard," I tell him.

Richard doesn't laugh. "You're better off without the job," he says. "But you should go and pick up your things today, especially since he's leaving." He pauses. "I wonder what he'll do with Barbara."

"Now we've got the whole summer together," I say.

I can hear what sounds like surf through Richard's phone. "Carrie, I'm glad you're here," he says. "But be sure to get your stuff. Owen's likely to sink it at high tide."

I imagine my backpack settling into the clam flats and I laugh, then Richard laughs too. I feel that happy suspension again, our laughter lifting me up into the heart of the summer day.

I push the black button imprinted with a white crescent moon and listen to the bell jangle in the hall.

I peer into a casement window at the side of the door. Through the diaphanous curtain I can identify a striped towel draped on the black incurvated banister.

I pull on the aluminum screen door; it sticks then shudders open. Listening for a swish of movement in the house, I lift the dulled brass knocker and rap three times on its plate. I hear the crash and chime of something breaking, and I hold my breath.

I let the door sigh closed, then, standing with my arms akimbo, I listen hard, the chirr of insects unnaturally loud. The skin on the back of my neck suddenly prickles and I jump from the porch. I jog to the beach, try to skip smooth stones, and watch a pair of catamarans sculling through a squall.

*   *   *

75

Richard opens the bottom drawer of his bureau and digs through piles of old clothes. "Here you go, Cunningham. Try these on for size."

He tosses me a pair of worn olive-colored jeans and a sailor-striped T-shirt. "They'll do fine," I say.

Richard stands and turns, then pins a red fishnet T-shirt to my shoulders with his thumbs. He cocks his head and frowns. "Won't do, won't do at all." He strokes his chin. "A bit too risqué for Chebeague." He breaks into a slow grin, then, gathering the T-shirt into his crooked arm, he kisses me lightly on the cheek. "I bought this when you were in Europe," he explains. "Wanted to change my image." His smile fades. "Then I got the ferry job here and bought my first slicker."

I take a deep breath, impatient with the inevitability of the moment. "Richard," I say, "about Europe."

"No, please," he interrupts. "That was then and there. Perhaps we will rekindle things this summer. Let's just take it one day at a time."

I smile into Richard's puckered face, then listen to the susurration of leaves outside the opened window. "It's raining," I announce.

Richard looks out at the stone-colored sky, then shuts the bureau drawer with his knee. "I'll go bring in the mail," he says.

I follow him down the stairs then watch as he sprints across the puddled road to the mailbox.

Out of breath, he hands me a rain-spattered envelope, which I tear open to find a note scrawled in red magic marker. You've been warned, it reads. Get off the island while you can.

"Jeez," I say, trembling. "What a madman." I show the note to Richard.

Richard frowns, and pounds his fist against his thigh. "Don't pay any attention to this, Carrie," he says. "We'll show him. You just lay low awhile until this blows over."

The rain and a sudden stab of fear chill me, pimple my bare arms. I stand watching the rain, feel the floorboards shift below me, the house a precariously anchored vessel.

The next morning I wake late and greet Richard, white-faced in shaving cream, in the bathroom. "Do you think we should leave?"

I ask him.

Richard tilts his chin back and swipes at his throat, leaving pink scars in the foam. "Well, you suit yourself, but no, I don't, Carrie." He taps his razor against the sink and clouds of cream float on the streaming water. "Don't let anyone intimidate you," he says, staring at me in the mirror.

"Right," I say.

I pull my desk in front of my bedroom window and look up from my typing whenever a car rolls by. Soon, all the compact cars look like Subarus, and all the dark cars look gray.

Later that day, Richard drives me to the dockside store where I buy dusty cans of tomato sauce, english muffins, sardines in olive oil and a five pound bag of cat food. As we walk to the car with the groceries, Richard says, "Isn't that the Ficketts' car over there?"

I try to peer around a pick-up truck loaded with weather-beaten lobster traps, but can only see the brightwork of a fender and a stripe of metallic gray. I begin to walk quickly, feeling vulnerable in the fog.

Back home I suggest I return to Amherst for a few days.

"I was thinking we could go down to Amherst anyway to pick up the rest of your stuff," Richard says smiling.

I squint at him. "I don't know if I can stay here, Richard. I'm all adrift with the Fickett business."

"I thought you weren't letting it trouble you, Carrie. He can't stay mad over such a small matter for long."

"He frightens me. He's still touchy about you and his daughter."

"Can't we forget that now?"

"Sure, sure," I say. "But he hasn't"

"Look, the point is, are you going to move in here or not?" He runs a hand through his hair. "No, let me put it this way: I want you to move here. How 'bout it?"

All of the light in the dim room is concentrated on Richard's face, and I blink, trying to summon up the familiarity of our years or the desire that propelled me off of the Portland dock and onto Richard's boat. But I am left with a memory of Owen's pale face and the taste of fear like sulfur on my tongue.

"I don't know," I say truthfully. "I did for awhile, but now I don't know.

"Carrie," he begins, then moves out of the light toward me. We hear a flump on the porch. Richard strides to the door and creaks it open. "What the hey," he says, and steps out.

When I join him, he is crouched over the cat's stiff body, checking it for wounds. "Poison?" he wonders.

"No," I say incredulously. "Would Owen do such a thing?" I kneel on the warped wood and feel tears break in my throat.

Richard goes inside to make some phone calls. I watch the wind riffle the cat's dark fur, then cover her with a piece of white canvas.

In the morning, Richard wakes early — I hear the squeak of his boat shoes against the wooden stairs. I watch him from my upstairs window; he loads newspapers and a round red can of gasoline into the trunk of his car.

Alarmed, I dress quickly. When I reach the porch, I see his car turning toward Fickett's house. I find a bike propped against the railing, then pump after him, my breaths moist and sharp in the damp morning air.

Richard sees me in his rearview mirror; he brakes and pulls over to wait for me.

"Richard," I say, gasping, when I reach him. He has rolled down his window, pulled his trucker's hat over his eyebrows. Something about the way he juts his jaw and presses his lips frightens me — Richard looks fanatical. "Let's go for a bike ride," I insist. "Why don't you turn around and we can take a morning ride."

Richard looks down the road, then up at me. His face softens. "Sure," he says, adjusting the side view mirror. "As you like."

After we circle the island on bikes, Richard leads me to the beach as a lavender mist shrouding the far islands rolls across the bay. Richard dives into the cold water; the ripples from his submersion jostle a rubber raft supporting two giggling girls with close-cropped hair and pierced ears.

I grow fidgety after an hour. The air is redolent with sun-dried kelp and brine. My muscles are rigid, tense; my legs feel like starched cords. If Richard touched me now, I might curl up and sink into the warm sand, fearing the consequences. Finally I say to Richard, wet from the recent plunge, "Let's get out of here."

He watches a small black dog race an incoming wave, then

agrees, "Okay."

As we cycle up the gravel driveway to Richard's I imagine other scenes of disaster: Richard's punt sunk past the clam flats; the Galaxie's tires punctured; Owen's house ablaze. I tramp up the the house, wipe my thonged feet carefully, then climb the stairs to my room to pack my diminished belongings.

Richard stands in the doorway and wipes his forehead against his sleeve of his polo shirt. "Do you want me to come with you?"

I am struck by the generosity and desperation of his offer, but want nothing now except to return to that moment of suspension back on the Portland dock when all my desires were as clear and compelling as instincts. "No," I say to Richard. "Massachusetts is not good for you."

He nods for a long time. I hand him a sheaf of papers. "Here's my story. Finished it last night. You're in it," I add mischievously. I fish in my tote bag and check the ferry schedule.

"I'll drive you to the two o'clock boat," Richard offers.

"Thanks," I say. "And thanks for everything." I reach out for Richard, kiss, then hug him, full of regret that for all of our intentions, forces beyond our control have left our desire unconsumed and unconsummated.

As Richard drives me to the dock, we listen silently to Kenny Rogers sing "The Gambler" on the car radio. Before I board the boat floating low on the neap tide, I clasp Richard's hand.

"You've got a good firm handshake, Cunningham," he says admiringly. "It's sure to get you places."

"Richard," I state, then swallow the words I want to say: I'm sorry. I'm scared. I want to love you. On the docked boat, I settle myself beside a stocky man guarding a set of barbells and wave to Richard as the ferry pulls out into Casco Bay.

I sit back and let the sun warm my face until we cruise past a granite jetty. I have overlooked or underestimated everything that mattered this summer: my uncertainties, Mrs. Fickett's needs, Mr. Fickett's malevolence, Richard's heartbreak. These five days have been too long and too short. I rummage in my canvas tote for a postcard; I decide to write down everything I didn't say to Richard and send it to him soon. I am sure he doesn't understand why I left. I can't find any postcards, but recognize a sheet of typing paper. With an involuntary groan, I pull out the last page of my story, and watch it luff in the wind.

CANDY

1. Candy

WHEN YOU OPEN THE DOOR, smelling of the bourbon and beer you had on the way home from work, you see Candy just rising out of bed, looking steamy and tropical. She's wearing an old red slip with black lace fringing her young damp breasts. One silk strap twists down loose over her left shoulder. Her eyes are dark and mascara-smeared. Somebody on the radio is singing, "Breath's on fire, don't touch me, I'm a real live wire." Candy puts on her sunglasses, picks up a can of warm beer from beside the bed, pops it open, licks the froth bubbling out, and pads into the bathroom. You peel off your T-shirt, wash your face in the kitchen sink, and lean out the window, but the heavy late afternoon heat doesn't dry you off. You watch an old man's shoes sink in the soft tar in the alley; everything is silent and hot until a bleating siren punctures the heat and you draw your head back into the kitchen. "Better run run run run run run run away." When the phone rings and the song ends, Candy takes off her sunglasses to coat your cheeks with kisses. Your hair gets curlier and curlier; your skin shimmers like napalm in the heat. She lets the phone ring, and waits. When the sun goes down, she keeps the lights off, the radio on, and you are left staring at one another in the hot dark stillness, slivers of wood in your elbows from the rough windowsill. A bass throbs, a drum beat stings, but Candy still waits. Candy waits until the only thing you can see is the orange glow of the radio. She flicks on the bathroom light, and in its yellow halo she daubs her lips with lipstick, rubs her cheeks with rouge until they look punched. When you and Candy walk down to the railroad tracks, ooh, baby, she says, the sky's on fire. When you slip your hand down her unzipped pants, she digs her fingernails into the back of your neck, bites your shoulder and leaves toothmarks in the skin. Get wet, you say, and she spreads her legs on the bright humming rails. She can feel the shimmy of the train through the warm steel. You lean down on top of her, push her face against the sooty gravel. She looks down the blue track as if it were the the barrel of a gun. Her pants are crumpled down around her knees. Her throat is feverish and pink, her hips cool and sheened in sweat. She screams; the train is going sixty.

2. Just Another Night Out

Candy is the salad girl. She tucks a lavender handkerchief soaked in Eau de Love cologne into her peasant blouse. Old-fashioned silk stockings with seams crawl up her sunburned legs and make her look even younger than eighteen. She teeters across the black and white checkered floor on patent leather platform shoes. Angie, the old blue-haired waitress, chuckles behind her back, and adds escarole to Candy's frowsy salads.

You come in during break wearing your paint-spattered smock. Candy eats day-old pizza and reads get-rich-quick schemes from matchbooks to the shy dishwasher. You order a glass of cheap red and shake parmesan cheese onto your garlic bread.

Angie, smiling wisely, brings you change; you lean over the jukebox, drop a quarter in the coin slot to play songs you think might get Candy going. You find her behind the cash register singing along with Elvis Presley. Her sleepy eyes make you want to move; you want to play Hound Dog all night long. Dance? you ask, stretching out your arms.

No time to dance, she says and smooths her stockings up over her knees.

Oh, c'mon honey. You gotta dance; you're Ann-Margaret, Eva Marie Saint.

Tell me more, she says. She hooks her arms around your neck and closes her eyes. You pull her up to dance closer to the warm machine.

Angie sets a plate of hot vermicelli at your table, and scolds Candy to sign out before dancing. Candy spins away from you to count her tips at your table. She lights a cigarette.

Your breath is careful and slow; shadows move across her face as a candle in a bowl flickers. More? you ask.

What, says Candy, smashing her cigarette in a puddle of red wine. More what?

While Angie fills sugar bowls in the back, Candy punches open the cash register and folds a thin stack of tens into her lavender handkerchief. You meet at the door. A bell tinkles as you leave.

Do you want more? you ask as Candy walks beside you. You can hardly breathe the words.

3. Thursdays

On Thursday, Candy turns her face from the wall to look at you. You are surrounded by books and paper, chalk and paint. All of the light in the room is bluish, dusty. Candy pours herself a glass of milk from the jug on your desk, then lies on a gessoed canvas and asks you to hold her bare feet in your ink-stained hands. Blowing softly on her naked legs, you watch all the tiny blonde hairs prick up. With every touch, you and Candy grow lighter, plumes of smoke in the light. Only wisps of vapor now, you twine together like numbus fog. When it begins to rain, you are thirsty for the milk. A lone fly paddles on its surface, makes thick white ripples in the jug. You drink the milk anyway. Squeezing a bottle of glue, Candy prints her name on the cover of your sketchbook.

Thursday morning, waking from a dream of tunnels, Candy hugs you hard and licks circles in your ear. There are dark half moons under your eyes; your lips are thick with sleep, but you roll over and drape your arm across her back. Mmmm, ahh, you could do it in your sleep, but the cats spring up on the bed, walk up and down your legs, knead their claws into your stomachs. You get up, pull on a bathrobe, pour cat food into their bowls, shut the door and climb back into the bed, still warm. Toes cold, breasts soft, morning rain, hands, hands, mmmm, ahh, you could do it in your sleep, but the neighbor kids pound at the door, yank it open and twirl paintbrushes. Get up, get dressed, raincoats, dry socks, toast and coffee, no milk, army men on the dining room table. You can't play baseball in the rain, so you take the neighbor kids to the aquarium instead. Candy sits at the window dressed in a long football jersey. She paints her toenails pearly pink, then blows on the polish until it dries.

It is Thursday when the summer ends and Candy squints behind her sunglasses as you kiss her powdered shoulder. Your moustache is wet and white with milk as you dress to leave; your hair is as dry as a coconut shell. You close the door and listen to Candy slide the bolt into place. You wait until reedy music swirls through the keyhole like water in scotch. Rushing downstairs, you look up at your window where a shadow dances behind the sheer curtain. Midnight music leaks through the window, but you cannot make out the tune. The sun suddenly tumbles from behind the clouds, and all you can see now is cirrus white and morning blue. Later, you come home to a note painted with nail polish, and look for footsteps in the chalk dust on your studio floor.

4. Want You Back in my Arms Again

Candy sees you watching her in the reflection of the window. When you woke up this morning, your skin was scored from the creases in the sheets and the rubble of her bones in the bed. Candy drinks cranberry juice in the sun, smashing mosquitoes against the glass. Across the alley, through the humming staffs of telephone wires and laundry rope, Stephanie dances to old Supremes songs, mouthing the words in the mirror, twitching her shoulders and rocking her hips to Baby, baby, where did your love go. Candy closes her eyes, swings her arms, and snaps her fingers with the drumbeat. You hang over the foot of the bed and flip through a movie catalog, making wishes that will never come true.

When Candy's breath fogs the glass, she traces delicate eighth notes in the condensation. You watch her shadow sway in a shard of sun against the wall, then you roll onto your back, making stars on the ceiling with Candy's hand mirror, hoping Candy will read your signals. You have never felt so scared, nor so young.

Shimmying into the kitchen, Candy hums along with Aretha Franklin shouting, What you want, baby I got it. You bump the refrigerator, and glossies of Candy's favorite stars flutter down; you two-step around the bed on all the wrong beats and think, all she wants is a spangled dress and a microphone. All you want is to stop your bones from breaking and clacking like beads inside your chest. All she wants is to turn up the stereo a little louder. All you want is to be sixteen, whistling the harmony with your hand down Candy's pants.

5. Sirens

I'm off to study the Trojan Wars, Candy says over the thutter of her engine. You stare at a stack of books lashed onto a chrome fender, and imagine the smell of the sea in her hair. Wait for me, she commands. I'll be back. Truth is, Candy has given up to join a lesbian motorcycle gang. Prerequisites are black leather stiletto-heeled boots and breasts that can cut like daggers. Candy swivels about, slashing opponents at chest level before they know what hits them. The Eighties are tough, she reminds them. After raising hell, leaving streaks of oil and strips of rubber on the streets, Candy's gang goes to the deli to sip cherry cokes through paper straws and read *True Confession* magazine. They tell wild lies to the waitresses to explain their leather jackets and tight silk pants stained with oil: Candy is a metermaid, Stephanie makes TV movies about truckers, Ingrid is from Saudi Arabia. They steal all the copies of *Hot Rodder* and *Star* that they can stuff down their pants. Stephanie wears a skirt, hooks adventure comics and romances on her garters. The cops come after them, lights flashing, sirens moaning, but they disappear on the street, climb down manholes, hold their breath as the sludge flows by. They wander around in the pipes, peek through sewer gratings, then emerge on the strange streets littered with crumpled newspapers. The real fun comes when they bind Candy to her handlebars with greasy bicycle chains and Stephanie reads, reciting the words from the magazines. Stephanie puts beeswax in her ears, Candy writhes about, dreaming of gypsies. They never come home.

WORDS OF LOVE

1.

FIRST THING HE SAYS when I get home from work is, "Don't talk to me." Says it from the kitchen where I know he's hunched over his books, jaw muscles twitching from too much coffee. I stand in the front hall, fingers combing through the heft of my new haircut. This isn't unusual, this brash candor, and I'm getting tired of words anyway, so I turn on the radio, pinch dry leaves curled on the ivy vines.

At the kitchen table in the dead fluorescent light, Drew is holding his forehead with the palm of his hand. He is barechested despite the snow outside, and his skin is pale, shadowed with purple. I wrap my fingers around his neck, rub the skin between his shoulders, and watch the muscles cleave under my thumbs. He pulls away and gives me a cartoon look of terror. "Don't you come near me. Don't touch me," he says. In a comic strip, his balloon would read, "Yikes!" He makes a gun out of a rubber band and aims it at my breasts, then returns to the hieroglyphics of his graphs and formulas. I look at the back of his head and think, I could hate this man.

But I don't. We have said that love and other bonds stronger than love keep us together, morning after morning. This usually consoles me, but today the old doubts begin, and I crouch next to Drew, look at his familiar big hands and wrists. "We need to talk," I state. I want to hear him say I shouldn't worry; he will love me for the rest of our lives, morning after morning.

Instead, he says, "Not interested."

"Not interested," I repeat. "That's a fine response. What *does* interest you these days?"

"Heisenberg," Drew claims, tapping the page with his forefinger. He bends forward and recites an equation quietly, moving his lips.

2.

The second time I ever made love with Drew, I knew we'd be lovers a long time. On a hot July evening, gnats like steam in the tree shadows, Drew picked me up in his mother's station wagon. We had rolled around on secluded damp park lawns a few days before; I found tiny bruises the twigs had made on the soft white skin of my upper thighs. But we were still shy with one another, especially since Drew was younger, still in high school. With melodramatic self-importance, we were secretive, and we maintained a charade of indifference; people we still know from those days are surprised to discover we were sweet on each other then.

Like tourists, we drove along the lakefront gawking at the waves, chaotic jazz I didn't like playing on the tape deck. We sat far apart, staring at the grassy median strips and our clumsily large hands. When we headed for Lake Park, Drew pulled out a bottle of warm pink wine from under the front seat. I was ascetic in those days, eating only fruits and grains and fresh vegetables, and I snorted, told him to drink it alone somewhere else, we didn't need that phony stimulation. God, I was hard on him then in a way I could never be now; he's no longer soft and fuzzy with awe for me; my conventionality seems safer and more calculated, and he's heard all my lines, seen my resolve go slack as I've aged and settled for pleasures rather than ideals.

Once it grew dark, we circled the northern suburbs, conversing disjointedly, distracted by trying to find a spot where we could park the car and make love. We'd already decided to fold down the back seat — all we needed was a place secluded enough. Finally, as I impatiently rolled the electric windows up and down, punched the cigarette lighter, we turned into the parking lot of my high school. We smiled at one another. The handrest between us seemed mountainous. Drew climbed into the back and spread a beach blanket over the rough carpeting.

Very softly, Drew said, "Anna, get back here. And take that crazy scarf off of your hair."

Easily scrambling over the seat in the dark, I thought about my choir teacher, Mr. Magnoli, how we were parked in front of his room. Drew cupped his hands over my shoulders. In the darkness, I saw his eyes shining with a funny sacred-candle sort of light, and I unzipped my pants, rolled his shorts off his ankles, closed my eyes and found his lips in the hot dark stillness.

Our bodies twined together effortlessly, breath fogged the windows, laughter leaked through the doors. The car rocked and swayed as if it'd been hit broadside. In the middle of a song of moans and coos, a dog barked nearby and someone rapped on the driver's window. I remembered Mr. Magnoli again, and shivered, releasing Drew.

Drew hunted for his shorts, finally covered himself with the corner of the blanket, and tried to roll down the window, but no go, the switch clicked ineffectually. Drew threw my jeans to me, then wiped a hole in the condensation and yelled, "Excuse me, mister."

The dog yapped and leaped up against the fender. Stone cold suburban father shook his head, memory of adolescence dead. He motioned gravely toward the parking lot exit.

Drew exaggerated the words. "We were just leaving." I muffled my laughter by holding my crumpled pants to my mouth, sore from kissing.

"Get your filthy hides away from here," the man said loudly, attaching his dog to the leash. "Park it somewhere else."

"Right," Drew yelled. "Just let me get my pants on."

The man stood, impassively watching the droplets of condensation thicken and roll until we tooted and roared off, choking and giggling about filthy hides, a new addition to our shared vocabulary, a future code phrase for furtive sex.

We held hands, our fingers remembering. "Drew," I said, blinking in the buzzing blue lights of the streetlamps, "we have just had an all-American experience." I squeezed his right knee, and he accelerated, racing shadows.

3.

For the third time today, I have parsed one simple sentence, trying to reduce the words to a collection of morphemes and glossemes, the smallest components of meaning. "Write loyal cantons of contemned loved," Shakespeare mysteriously wrote. Alicia, my co-worker, has already provided accurate etymologies of the words, but prefixes and roots lie scattered like jigsaw puzzle pieces on my paper. Dictionaries and textual glosses obscure and reduce the meaning, not elucidate it. The sentence anyway means more than the sum of its words, but I don't know the formula for this multiplication.

I stare at the word "love" until it is reduced to an analphabetic series of letters, then mere converging and diverging lines, no more illuminating to me than Babylonian cuneiform. Lately, this reduction happens far too often; sometimes I look at my own name and see only a palindrome. I wonder how much longer I can work as a linguist. Once, I reveled in the labyrinths of words; dissecting them made their talismanic powers clear. Now, the more I look for the magical bonds between glyph and meaning, the more indecipherable even the simplest words become.

The same frustrating blindness pervades the rest of my life. Everything that matters to me seems to be expressed in some kind of code for which I lack the key. Drew reminds me that some things can only be understood obliquely, but I want a Rosetta stone that will make it all clear.

I tack the Shakespeare quotation to my bulletin board, and head for my shelf of old dictionaries. I want to concentrate on etymologies awhile. It's the only linguistic task I enjoy anymore, sifting through archaic tracts and ancient documents to discover the earliest forms and usages of a word. History at least can occasionally explain the gibberish with which we define ourselves.

4.

Sometime during our fourth year together, after watching our romantic illusions evaporate, replaced by a friendly familiarity, Drew and I decided to move in together in Madison.

Late that first night in our new flat, I unpacked books in the dining room, happily shuffling Drew's fiction into my own. Drew, smirking beneath a Brewer's baseball cap, held Paya, my cat, and paced, proclaiming that he had loved me first.

"Oh yeah? Prove it," I said offhandedly.

Visor cocked, Drew toed a pile of paperbacks I'd been hauling around for years. "Look on page sixteen in one of those anthologies," he said.

Enjoying the banter, I made a suspicious, weary face.

"Don't give me that look, just check it out. It's on the bottom of the page."

I systematically flipped through books until I found a string of capital letters at the bottom of a page sixteen. A code. "Okay, smartie. What's it say?" I pushed the book into his chest. I recognized it as a collection I had lent him years ago.

"You're the linguistics major," he claimed. "You figure it out."

I puzzled over the senseless letters until I understood they were written in Double Dutch. Translated, they read, "We shall be married."

I smiled and closed my eyes. "That'll be the day," I said, teasing, feeling sassy and hopeful.

Drew gestured expansively. "Anna, you silly. We're already on the way."

I looked up expecting to see Drew smirking at the joke, but his smile was placid and serious. "How do you know all of this?" I said, suddenly sad. "I've been trying to gain that certainty you have for years."

He rubbed Paya's ears. "You try too hard, Anna," he claimed. "You can't know everything at once. In the end, all you'll know is *how* you understand us."

We'd spent most of the previous months sitting across from one another at restaurant tables and booths, talking until our tongues were dry. This is how the most of our conversations ended. "Please, Drew. Spare me."

He laughed and set the cat down, then pulled me close, patting me on the back. When he kissed my ear, tears broke in my throat. Drew wasn't generally affectionate with me — I'd come to interpret any small physical gesture as a demonstration of love.

I still have that book, a collection of contemporary American fiction. Inevitably, I will wrap it in bright paper and present it to Drew, but not yet. The code will only make us marvel at the changes.

Then, will and the mystery of love determined the future. Now, it is the past which binds us.

5.

It is already January fifth, and I can't sleep; the cold is distracting me. Watching headlights sparkle and fade in the frost braided on the window, I'm thinking of having an affair. Drew and I haven't had sex since before Christmas, way before. I've watched for clues to explain his lack of interest, but he's simply distant, preoccupied with his studies. The problem is, I don't know anyone I could sleep with. I've been reclusive this winter. I could get out and about more, but the other problem is that Drew probably wouldn't be threatened if I did have an affair. He'd be tolerant, relieved. It's Drew I want anyway, the peace in belly as he lays his head between my breasts to listen for my heartbeat.

Here is the fantasy to which I fall asleep: Drew comes to bed damp from the shower, slips under the quilt to hold me, then asks me riddles and brain teasers. I know all the answers. We are laughing, the lights fade yellow, and I am warm in the circle of his arms, warm and sleepy watching the windows shake as the wind blows. We wake in the weak winter sun, still entangled, sharing dreams.

The sound of Drew's boots clomping on the hardwood floor awakens me. I've been listening for it, and I hold the covers above my head.

"Get your filthy hide in here, Drew, and we'll cuddle," I say.

He is lost in the pleasure of rubbing his feet; his teeth are clenched, eyes focused on something beyond this room. His self-containment makes him look alien to me; even his face and limbs seem unfamiliar.

"I'm tired, Anna, and it's late. I'm going to sleep."

I let the covers float down around me. I don't want Drew to see my flushed, pinched face. I massage his scalp and whisper, "Hold me, Drew."

Drew lies on top of the quilt, arms pinned under his chest and hips. Already he begins his measured breathing.

"C'mon, Drew," I plead, tugging at the sheet. I think of the magician's trick of pulling a tablecloth out from under an elegantly-set table.

I want to tickle him until he is awake. "Drew, I have to talk to you," I say urgently. I turn on the light and sit up.

"Okay, Anna, talk." Half of Drew's mouth is flattened against the mattress and his whole face looks distorted. I interpret his actions: he is not tired, but fatally bored with me.

"Sit up," I say, my voice shaky with fear and anger.

I listen to the ticking and creaking of the walls. Drew sighs. "I'm listening. Talk."

I pound my fist against his shoulder. "Sit up at least. You can hardly hear me."

Drew rolls over and stretches out on his back. "I can hear you just fine." He rubs his shoulder.

I cover my cold feet with the hem of my flannel nightgown. "Listen," I say. "We've got to talk this out." He closes his eyes. "It's just that it's winter and I'm lonely and need some reassurance."

I wait for him to say the magical words which will invoke serenity, but he only drapes his forearm over his eyes, and asks, "Could you turn out the light?"

I scramble down the mattress, hook my knee over Drew's leg and lay my head on his bicep. "Do you love me?" I ask fiercely. "That's what I want to know." Slipping my hand under his T-shirt, I trace the bones of his chest, blind fingers groping for braille.

Drew rubs his eyes, and lets them focus on the ceiling. "I'll never answer that."

"What does *that* mean?" I sit up, hair falling dramatically. I am flushed with the kind of indignant anger I know will make Drew freeze up and withdraw.

"Love is a word," he explains and looks at me. "I'm here. Everything else that matters," and here he pauses to juggle air, "is ineffable. Spelling it out reduces things." Drew clutches the covers and raises them over our shoulders, holds me until he twitches in his sleep and his arms slip away.

I still can't fall asleep. The word ineffable baffles me; how can a word describe the indescribable? I turn off the lamp and stare at stilted tree shadows like Runic writing on the walls. I disagree with

Drew. Love is a paradox; the more you reach out for it, the more it recedes from you. I want to explain this to him, and I think about waking him up. I'll begin: if we love each other, then why am I not happy?

6.

During our sixth summer together, Drew and I flew to Europe. Midway through the trip, we tired of major cities and museums, and decided to rest in a nearly-deserted youth hostel in southern Italy. The trilingual proprietor, Signor Pei, struck a curious bargain: we could stay in his hostel, a crumbling 14th century castle, for a reduced rate if we studied Italian with him. Naturally, we agreed, though he proved to be a dogmatic and impatient teacher. He scoffed at our pronunciation, and denounced the American educational system because we could not memorize long recitations easily. I grew irritated with him except during lessons, while Drew remained amused.

In order to avoid Signor Pei's intrusions, Drew and I would quiz one another and practice grammar and vocabulary on the beach. The village children, shielded from the sun in American baseball caps, would ring our blanket, encourage our Italian-esque stutterings, and ask us for definitions in English. They taught us every Italian hand signal they knew.

One morning Signor Pei greeted us as we prepared to descend to the beach. He smiled at the Italian dictionary and text tucked into my straw bag.

"And to where are you headed," he asked us in English. Drew fumbled with a response in Italian, but I interrupted. "We're going to conjugate on the beach," I said, not picking up the double entendre.

Drew began to laugh, then stopped when he saw Signor Pei's rubescent face. Signor thrust a train schedule at Drew, and commanded us to leave the village *immediatamente*.

Puzzled, I watched Signor Pei retreat into the castle. Drew had to pull me down the rocky path to the train station.

"Conjugate," Drew explained, "has more than one definition."

"Right," I replied defensively. Until Signor Pei's indignant response, I had only fuzzily guessed at the word's second definition. "He must have known we were going to conjugate verbs, not our bodies."

"You assume too much," Drew said. "You never know what someone else thinks a word means."

I scrambled down the scree and waited for Drew on the street. "That's nuts," I said. "We might as well say nothing at all."

"Right," Drew said lightly. "Words are just tricks anyway."

7.

Today is the seventh day since my awkward late-night encounter with Drew, and I'm taking refuge from the empty sad hours by trying to be productive in my office. Lately, nothing Drew says makes me feel secure.

We had another silly fight yesterday, something I provoked out of frustration, and even after the argument had run its course, I was still fretting that fundamentals were really at issue. I retreated to the bathroom, where Drew found me vigorously scrubbing out the bathtub, face pinched and red with tears.

"Anna," he said softly, concerned. He took the sponge out of my hand, held me by the shoulders and steered me to the toilet. He daubed at my face with tissue, then sat on the bathtub ledge and waited for me to stop sobbing.

"No," I said, trying to steady my voice. "Don't you see?" A freshet of tears soaked the pink tissue. "It's not what you say, but what you don't say. You're going to leave me."

Drew shook his head and squeezed my knee. "Is that what you think? Don't you know how I feel?"

"No, I don't," I whispered angrily. "That's the point."

Drew gently pulled me to the bathtub, and held me until the porcelain grew too cold on our bare legs.

Now I riffle the pages of a volume of my Oxford English Dictionary and squint at the blackboard where Alicia has left me a message: Check for acronyms. Word order is important. Once I would have scoured a text with mathematical precision, ferreting out the subtext which confirms meaning flickering behind the words like so much ultra-violet light, undetected by the unaided human eye. Instead, I am disappointed with words and prefer to mull over other mysteries. What is it that keeps Drew and me together? History? Habit? Inertia? If it is love, the most bewildering of bonds, then how do I overlook the small cues and understated codes that could let me undoubtedly know this is love? Would I know anymore if Drew frequently declared it?

Drew doesn't seem to be troubled by doubts. Is this arrogance? Or is his apparent reticence an indication of his unconditional love? I only wish the words that express love were magical, an incantation that could transform my doubts into sure knowledge, that it would only be a matter of Drew uttering them.

It is getting dark now though it is only late afternoon, and I am getting nowhere. The peacefulness I desire with Drew seems more elusive than ever, and my dictionary seems only a collection of letters. My first impulse is to stare at the pages until the definitions are clear, but I am eventually drawn to the dark window where I can see the stubble of the snowless ground under the streetlights. Raising my eyes, I pick out what I think is the Northern Star, then wait to make a wish, but the words never come.

8.

This is our eighth year together, and Drew has been unfaithful to me twice, both during a summer when I took graduate level classes at Cambridge, England. I was sitting on my bed in Cambridge, listening to the rain, when I read Drew's letter explaining how he had slept with Corrine, a mutual friend. They were both drunk and seduceable, he explained. I wondered first if seduceable were indeed a word, then remembered Corrine's long dancer's legs. I dieted and biked everywhere for the rest of the summer.

I returned to Madison from Cambridge a few days early to surprise Drew. I caught a bus near the airport, then walked to our apartment, trembling and smiling. I opened the door, looked in all the rooms and closets, then decided to take a bath and wait for Drew. The familiar sight of our towels and furnishings pleased me.

At five p.m., I made a pan of manicotti and warmed it in the oven. At seven, I left to buy a bottle of wine, sure that Drew would be home when I returned. Instead, the apartment was dark and cool, and I opened the Chianti, then changed into something close-fitting and black. After all that biking, I felt fit and desirable. By nine, I was drunk and scared, inventing implausible excuses for Drew's absence. I fell asleep for a short time, awakening when I heard a neighbor coming home from the bars.

When Drew finally arrived the next morning, he found me scraping the dark, dry manicotti into the sink. I had not slept more than an hour or so. Drew told me I looked skinny and did not hold me.

"Momentum," he explained later. Momentum was building with him and his new friend, Laurie. I did not need a dictionary to understand what "new friend" meant.

"Laurie or me," I declared, my eyes burning. I had so much to tell Drew about my summer, words I knew would bind us together.

"Give me some slack here," he said. "I need some slack." I left town and visited my parents, wrote long letters to Drew I never sent. After two weeks, Drew called me and told me Laurie was sweet, but didn't know how to talk. I came home, thin and pale. I will not endure this again, I said. Drew surprised me by accepting those words without argument, then holding me all night while we reminisced. Remember that weekend in Door County when we slept under the pines, he began.

9.

Tonight is the ninth night Drew has been late coming home from his restaurant job. The first weekend, he called to say he was going out for drinks with the other bartenders. Then he simply didn't say anything when he rolled in late the next few nights. We fought — I used every argument that had ever worked before, then remembered Laurie and threatened to leave. "Is that what you want?" I asked. "I don't know," he said. For a moment, he looked as young and frightened as I felt.

Before he left tonight, he promised he'd be home early. But I saw that impatient, nearly wild look in his eyes, and I knew his promise was meaningless.

So I am packing a few things, preparing to stay with Alicia until I find another apartment. Over the last two weeks or so, I talked to all my old friends, rehearsed sure-fire speeches for Drew, then finally gave in to wordless anger. Tonight, I am ready to leave: I feel it in my bones.

I have been composing a final note to Drew all night, but there is finally nothing to say. Drew and words have both betrayed me — all those "talks" could not create permanent bonds. I should be devastated, but am instead relieved. It is a relief that I have sensed Drew's lack of desire all along, that his committment was as evanescent as his words. Drew has not denied me language, but the primitive, pre-lingual knowledge of love.

It is the heart of the night now, and very dark. I turn on all of the lamps — I want to leave the apartment ablaze with light. All of my actions seem right and sure, and I am giddy with their power. Moving to the dark window, I smile at the stars and moon, imperceptibly spinning, then rush down the stairs into the cold, feeling brash and naked.

HOLIDAYS

I PARK ACROSS THE STREET from my parents' house in Wisconsin and pretend I am approaching it for the first time. The lawn has just been trimmed; I notice that right away. The grass is neatly cropped and blond at the base of my father's prize saplings: his Carpathian walnuts, Italian dwarf plums and budding apricots. "The trees," my father objects whenever my mother talks about moving. "We can't up and leave before the trees hit their prime."

Erika opens the front door and I kick a blue croquet ball across the lawn. I can still hear the hum of the road in my ears, smell the sourness of asphalt in the folds of my sundress. "Captain says take three giant leaps forward," Erika commands dryly, then blows smoke rings through the screen.

Clutching a duffel bag and swinging my car keys, I scuff across the gravel driveway to the porch, then bow dramatically. My dress sticks to the back of my legs. "Hi Rik," I say, patting her pockets for a cigarette. "You're looking good." Rik has no sense of style. Today she wears a shapeless mint-green velour top with purple sweats.

When I find her pack of Camels, Rik flips her lighter to me. "Mom's going to drop when she sees you. She's been trying to reach you all morning. They're predicting tornados in Ohio, you know." I waver in the shadows on the porch. All I want is to find a hushed corner of the house where I can forget about things in Ohio.

"Merle?" My father emerges from the far end of the garage, and I hide the cigarette in the palm of my hand. "Are you supposed to be here *today*?" He hugs me roughly and squeezes my biceps. "Still doing those chin-ups?" he asks, smiling. Erika shrugs and fades into the hall. My father rubs some flat leaves under my nose. "Now that's oregano." He beams. I beam back. My father looks young in the afternoon light.

I follow him into the backyard where my mother stands on the deck in a pale linen suit. She is having some trouble fastening a charm bracelet onto her wrist. "Oh, Merle, honey," she says and leans over the railing to kiss me. The moistness of her lipstick on my cheek and the sudden recognition of her perfume calm the turbulence in my stomach, and I feel the stirrings of hunger for the first time in days. "Did you *drive*? Through the *night*? Honey, we heard there were tornados. Didn't you turn on the radio for the weather?" My mother frets when I drive from Ohio to Wisconsin alone. She had a dream once, she explained, but never related the contents. Now she warns me: The tolls! The construction! The rush-hour traffic in Chicago! Fly instead, honey, she always says. You hardly know you're moving. We'll pay for the ticket. I never call to tell her when I'm coming to visit anymore.

"Honey, I wish you had called. I'm ready already, but Joanne's making dinner. Something experimental — chicken curry, or chicken something. There's salad stuff if it doesn't work out." As I light my cigarette, I see Joanne through the kitchen window, talking on the phone with the cord wrapped across the refrigerator. "Is that Bill on the phone again?" my mother demands loudly. My sister Joanne has always managed to date men who are terrific telephone conversationalists.

"Why don't they just get married, then they can talk all the time?" my father mutters, pulling weeds from between the flagstones.

I grind my cigarette out on a wrought-iron chair; I'm a furtive smoker around my father. When I was fourteen, my best friend, Patti, and I met two senior boys during the half of a high school basketball game. They talked about how they'd probably both buy Corvettes someday, and drove Patti and me home after some smoking and drinking and necking. Having arranged to pick me up after the game, my father waited in the high school parking lot, long after the spectators and team had left. He was quietly disappointed when we talked the next morning, but he still drove me anywhere I needed to go. I've never openly smoked a cigarette in his presence since then.

My mother tucks her clutch purse under her elbow. Her smile is wide and red. "How 'bout you, Merle? When are you and Duncan getting married? I want some grandchildren here." Both of my parents put up quite a fuss when Duncan and I first moved in together. My mother threatened that I wouldn't be welcomed back in the house unless we were married. My father just stared at me, his face sagging with sadness and bewilderment. Duncan took my parents out to lunch and explained that he already considered us married; the wedding would be a mere formality. That made them more suspicious but less punitive, and surprised me. I didn't think I could feel married to Duncan until years after some kind of ceremony.

"Mom," I say and step forward. I watch my father push the blade of a shovel into the garden to break the dark soil. "Duncan and I broke up. He's moving out the end of May."

My mother's smile flattens, then she drops her purse on the picnic table and rushes down the steps of the deck to hold me. "Oh, Merle. Oh, honey."

The sureness of her hands in my hair and the musical scrape and ting of my father's shovel make me want to cry, but I've had enough of that. I grow drowsy in the waning sunlight. Imagining my old bedroom, dark and cool, I want to sleep as I haven't in weeks. "Can I come home for awhile?" I ask, my words muffled in the nap of my mother's jacket.

Erika persuades Joanne and me to go bar-hopping with her. "You're both getting old and lazy," she claims. "You've got to get out there if you want anything to happen." Erika is the youngest and most bull-headed of us all. One Easter, when she was a preschooler, Erika slipped out of the yard in her pajamas and straw Easter hat to head for church while the rest of us slept. My mother called the police and prayed to St. Jude, while my father circled the neighborhood in his station wagon, a baseball bat tucked under the front seat. When the police found Erika en route to mass, she refused to ride with them, and, having learned her lesson about the friendly stranger, threw pebbles at their hubcaps. The fuming officers followed her all over the neighborhood for hours until my father caught up with them, cheering her gumption.

At BarNone, Erika knows all the bartenders. "Yeah, we're sisters," she tells Sam, the owner. "Who do you think is the oldest?" Erika, Joanne and I smile at each other in the mirror behind the liquor bottles. The shadows on my face and my tightly braided hair make me look European.

Sam dunks mugs into soapy water and squints at us. "You. The brunette." He points to Joanne who fingers the ringlets of her new haircut.

"Nope," Erika says, and nods at me. "Cow eyes over here is

number-one sister." I roll my big eyes at Erika, swivel nervously on my wobbly stool.

Joanne counts her change stacked next to a coaster. "Do you have a quarter?" she asks. "Bill's expecting my call." Erika shakes her head. I drum my fingers on the linoleum bartop, spin one of Joanne's nickels. Erika catches the coin before it rolls into the cash register. "Jeez, Merle, sit still. You want to meet some men?"

"Sure," I claim.

"Then sit over here." She indicates the stool next to her. "It's magic. Works every time."

I switch seats. Shortly after Joanne returns, Bill appears. Sunburned in rugby shorts, he nuzzles the nape of Joanne's neck, admires the softness of her elbows. Erika jokes earnestly with the bartenders and slides me free drinks. I sit in the magic seat for hours and watch couples drift up to the jukebox.

A group of drunken young men stride into the bar and gather near the dartboard. One looks something like Duncan, and is, in fact, wearing a madras jacket like the one Duncan wore one spring. I stare at his profile, my stomach churning.

"Irresponsibility," Duncan explained when I asked what he thought he'd gain by breaking up. "I just want to be irresponsible awhile."

"Merle?" My mother is standing in the doorway of my bedroom. "Honey, it's nearly two. You shouldn't sleep so much."

I blink and scan the room. My hands are tightly fisted on my thighs. I have been dreaming of a cool green stillness. "Mom, I need the sleep," I mutter.

She pulls the sheets back and pushes my brambly hair off my cheek. "You're a beautiful girl, Merle," she states emphatically.

Later, I slide open the patio door and find Joanne sunning on the deck. "Let's play Scrabble," I say. Hanging baskets of impatiens have all bloomed abundantly overnight.

"I have to work at five," Joanne claims.

"Five? We're going to play Scrabble for three hours?" I sprinkle sandy soil from a geranium pot onto Joanne's oiled stomach. When Joanne and I were kids, we'd rig old sheets in the basement, pretend they were clouds or walls or sails for hours. It's been too long since I've enjoyed that suspension of time and place.

"Joanne," I whisper persuasively. I nudge my toe between the strips of plastic on her lounge chair.

Joanne casually brushes the geranium dirt away and twists a small diamond ring on her finger. She and Bill were engaged on Sunday. "C'mon, Merle," she says and flips over. "Go bother someone else."

Last summer Duncan and I played Scrabble or chess or gin rummy every evening. He was a frenetic and unconventional gamester, though I rarely bet with him. He called himself Dougan in those days. When we first met, he called himself Duggie. I appreciated his unpredictability and spontaneity, qualities I hoped would rub off on me. He dressed in outfits that were more like costumes, a different style or period each day. He sprouted beards and moustaches of varying lengths and shapes, then would impulsively shave off part or all of them. You can fall in love with a new man every week, he urged me. Instead, his changing guises eventually made me feel off-balance, dizzy. His face, with its shadows of old beards, looked blurred to me. "Risks," he would declare. "You've got to take risks in all the facets of your life."

I walk off and stand in the spray of the lawn sprinkler, hearing my pulse race. My best friend, Amy, called me from Ohio last night. "Would you go back to Duncan if you could?" she asked. "He's home from the east coast." Once I agreed to break up, Duncan decided to visit every major city between Atlanta, Georgia and Portland, Maine.

"I don't know," I answered honestly. "I thought I would, but now I don't know. All I want is to stay in one place awhile."

My mother finds me paging through a Sears catalog at the dining room table and asks me to help her shop for groceries. "Pick out whatever you like," she says.

When I was a child accompanying her to the store, my mother would let me choose any three items I fancied. Instead of Reese's peanut butter cups and Drumsticks, I chose mangoes and spaetzle and gefilte fish, fascinated by the exoticness of their names or labels. I vowed to eat a pomegranate every day. Lately, however, I've had bowls of cold cereal for nearly every meal.

In the supermarket, overwhelmed by the array of produce, I am stumped, unable to choose one head from the bountiful varieties of lettuce.

"Merle? Honey?" My mother catches me looking woeful and yellow under the fluorescent lights. She slides her shopping cart up to me and selects a jar of artichoke hearts stacked in front of the grapes. Duncan loves artichoke hearts, used them in omelets and sandwiches, saved the jars for wing nuts and tacks.

"It's rough, isn't it, Merle?" My mother's gaze is direct, her face soft with concern. All of her daughters are reflected in that face. "Your father and I just want you to be happy, but it must be rough right now." She presses her warm palm over my cold fingers. "It's like a little death, isn't it?"

We are frozen in the mirror above the iced vegetables. "Mom," I say, squinting into the basket. "It's silly, but Duncan loved artichokes."

I watch with complicated relief as she frowns and replaces the jar. When she turns to me, I smile, then begin to laugh, and she laughs too, our fluty voices echoing on the tiled floor.

I find my father napping on a camp stool at the edge of the garden. Sprawling in the sun, I chew the stalk of a long blade of grass, let the chirr of cicadas lull me.

"Merle Marie," he sings, opening his eyes. I was named for both his father and mother.

"Sleeping?" I ask.

He smiles. "No, just resting my eyes. It's more rejuvenating than sleep." He turns toward the kitchen when the phone rings. "Your cousin is supposed to call today from Lucca," he explains.

When Duncan called late last night, Joanne answered the phone. I didn't speak to him; I had little to say. "Tell him I've been sleeping for two weeks straight," I said to Joanne, rumpled in her bathrobe. We were finally having our Scrabble showdown.

" 'Travel,' " Joanne reported Duncan saying. " 'I've completely changed since my travels.' " Joanne tidied her tiles. "I think he wants to come back to you."

Erika appeared with a bowl of popcorn. "How did this whole thing get started, anyway? This break-up?"

Both Joanne and Erika watched me thoughtfully, munching their popcorn.

"It really started over Christmas," I explained, "and got worse over New Year's. I wanted to celebrate, establish some traditions. You know, make it feel like home. Duncan said I was being suburban. Then I started teaching second semester, and things were okay awhile." I paused, sucked on a popcorn kernel. "But Valentine's Day was really bad. So was Easter."

"Stripes, action, go," Duncan explained when I came home to find a corner of the living room painted in thin wiggling red stripes. I had just bought two wicker baskets, cellophane grass and an egg-dying kit, all of which Duncan scorned. That was Easter Sunday, two weeks before Duncan announced he wanted out.

"Holidays," I said to Joanne and Erika. "We just couldn't make it through the holidays."

My father rubs my knee, then stoops to examine frilled leaves of lettuce. "It's nice to have some time off, huh? Summer vacation." He whistles something classical and familiar. "Opera singer," he wrote on a document which asked what he hoped his infant daughter would grow to be.

"Dad," I ask. "How long have you and Mom been married?"

"Thirty-five years," he answers. He twists a small head of lettuce and hands it to me. "Thirty-five years."

I look out over the yard, notice all the shades of green.

"You're doing fine," my father reminds me. "Sometimes things just have to lie fallow awhile."

My sisters and I set the dining room table with care, rolling linen napkins in silver rings, dusting off crystal water goblets. It's the evening of my father's birthday. "Let's not go to any trouble for a change," my father had stated that morning. Who could take him seriously? We have been polishing the napkin rings and setting out the water goblets on birthdays for at least fifteen years.

I find a box of trick birthday candles, another tradition, and slip them under the cake platter. When I bought them earlier in the day, I ran into Patti, my old friend from high school.

"You're living at *home* for the summer?" she asked. "Isn't it driving you nuts?"

During college, I could only stay home for three consecutive days before I grew restless and cranky. "No," I say to Patti. "I'm happy just to take it easy for the summer. I'll head back to Ohio the week before I start teaching." That was the first I'd detailed my plans to anyone.

My mother carries a frittata and a basket of hot Italian bread to the table, where my father grins at his daughters.

"Here's to you," I say, raising my water glass and returning his smile.

Early this morning, my father woke me from an uncomfortable dream of Duncan, treated me to a cup of strong coffee, then drove us out the country to a small farm. While fronds of mist twisted over the fields, my father and I picked strawberries, staining our fingers and lips with their juice. "This is a celebration," he said, helping me tote the basket heaped with berries.

The doorbell rings. Erika rises and pivots in the light from the porch lamp. "Merle, I guess it's for you."

Duncan stands on the porch with his hands pushed in front pockets of his tight black pants. A sleeveless T-shirt printed with a red Japanese character completes his collegiate new wave outfit. The frame of the door and its screen make Duncan look sallow and short.

"Hello Duncan," I say. Behind me, my sisters are clearing the table, and my mother studs a fruit pie with candles.

"Come home," Duncan says. I see now that Duncan has gained weight; his pants are much too tight on him.

"Home?" I ask, my fingers pressed to the screen. "I am home." Duncan sits on the porch step, tosses stones on the driveway. "I'll hound you," he claims. He shades his eyes to stare at me. "You can't stay here forever. You'll rot."

I watch him shake pebbles in his palm like dice, then plunk them one by one onto the pile of stones. "Aren't you going to invite me in at least?" he says. "We should talk."

"It's my father's birthday," I explain.

"Yeah?" Duncan squints at me through a cloud of gnats, and pitches more stones onto the driveway. "Birthday cake and all that? C'mon, Merle."

"Oh, Duncan, you just don't get it." I watch a scrawl of heat lighting illuminate the eastern sky, then scrape my fingernails across the screen between us. "I *like* birthday cake and all that."

He scowls, then reaches down for more gravel. "A long talk. We'll take a walk and have a long talk."

I imagine Duncan and I setting off down the driveway and past the sleeping suburban houses and their damp lawns. I would have to stop by the creek and say, Here is where I fell off my bike and broke a rib and lay, hot with shame, until my father and cousin David, the object of my girlhood crush, found me in the wild grapevines. And there, that's the street where Joanne and Erika and I played Kick the Can on warm summer nights, and Monty, the paper boy, was forever trying to kiss me in our neighbors' backyards. But Duncan doesn't have the patience for reminiscence, and besides, I can see he means to do most of the talking.

I hear the rustle and crump of wrapped presents being stacked behind me, and I sigh. "Duncan, there's nothing more to say. You don't know me and I probably don't know you."

"I can't believe you're going to leave me sitting on this porch all night," Duncan claims, and shrugs in a way that once made me want to give him things, do him favors. But too much time has passed; the long slow days with my family have healed me; I'm not susceptible to Duncan anymore.

"Go home," I say. Duncan moves back to his car parked across the street and squints at me. Then he runs onto the freshly-mowed lawn and kicks a clump of dried grass at a dwarf plum tree. I return to the table where my mother frowns and Erika rolls her eyes in exasperation. I am shivering, as if chilled. "Close the door?" my father asks Joanne. I light the candles, slide the pie to the middle of table, and we all make double wishes as the candles sputter and reignite. We hear the faint sound of stones pinging against the screen door until it begins to storm, rain pulled to earth.

Late that night, after the rain has stopped, my father plays a recording of "La Traviata" and sits with me on the porch. We breathe the rain-washed air, and he tells me the story of when he performed the opera as tenor. "You were just a child, but your mother took you to one of the performances. It must have been around Christmas time, because I remember you were both wearing red velvet dresses. During the first act, whenever I began to sing, you'd cry, scream your head off. You sounded louder than I did. I was secretly proud of that, but your mother was frantic. During intermission, I came out front in my costume. The director was furious with me. But I held you and let you mess my makeup. I walked you all over the theater." My father stands and hands me a broom. "For the rest of the opera, you were fine. An angel." He goes into the garage and finds a dustpan. "I'll never forget that Christmas," he says. We sweep the stones from the driveway and the porch.

BIOGRAPHICAL NOTES

Lisa Ruffolo was born in Milwaukee and, except for a four-year period of nomadic wandering, has always lived in Wisconsin. She now resides in Madison, where she and a partner run a computer software business. She has also been a high school English teacher and currently teaches writing part-time at the University of Wisconsin. She studied fiction writing with John Barth, Kelly Cherry, and Janet Shaw. *Holidays* is her first book.

Kathryn Wright has a degree in art and art history, and she has also studied anthropology, archeology, and commercial art. She exhibits her work in one person and group shows from time to time. Observing wild life and exploring wilderness and natural areas occupies a great deal of her time. She lives in Madison, Wisconsin with her two children and three cats.